PRAISE FOR THE D

Here are some of the over 100,000 five star reviews left for the Dead Cold Mystery series.

"Rex Stout and Michael Connelly have spawned a protege."

AMAZON REVIEW

"So begins one damned fine read."

AMAZON REVIEW

"Mystery that's more brain than brawn."

AMAZON REVIEW

"I read so many of this genre...and ever so often I strike gold!"

AMAZON REVIEW

"This book is filled with action, intrigue, espionage, and everything else lovers of a good thriller want."

AMAZON REVIEW

MUSTANG SALLY
A DEAD COLD MYSTERY

BLAKE BANNER

RIGHTHOUSE

Copyright © 2024 by Right House

All rights reserved.

The characters and events portrayed in this ebook are fictitious. Any similarity to real persons, living or dead, is coincidental and not intended by the author.

No part of this book may be reproduced in any form or by any electronic or mechanical means, including information storage and retrieval systems, without written permission from the author, except for the use of brief quotations in a book review.

ISBN-13: 978-1-63696-020-3

ISBN-10: 1-63696-020-0

Cover design by: Damonza

Printed in the United States of America

www.righthouse.com

www.instagram.com/righthousebooks

www.facebook.com/righthousebooks

twitter.com/righthousebooks

DEAD COLD MYSTERY SERIES
An Ace and a Pair (Book 1)
Two Bare Arms (Book 2)
Garden of the Damned (Book 3)
Let Us Prey (Book 4)
The Sins of the Father (Book 5)
Strange and Sinister Path (Book 6)
The Heart to Kill (Book 7)
Unnatural Murder (Book 8)
Fire from Heaven (Book 9)
To Kill Upon A Kiss (Book 10)
Murder Most Scottish (Book 11)
The Butcher of Whitechapel (Book 12)
Little Dead Riding Hood (Book 13)
Trick or Treat (Book 14)
Blood Into Wine (Book 15)
Jack In The Box (Book 16)
The Fall Moon (Book 17)
Blood In Babylon (Book 18)
Death In Dexter (Book 19)
Mustang Sally (Book 20)
A Christmas Killing (Book 21)
Mommy's Little Killer (Book 22)
Bleed Out (Book 23)

Dead and Buried (Book 24)
In Hot Blood (Book 25)
Fallen Angels (Book 26)
Knife Edge (Book 27)
Along Came A Spider (Book 28)
Cold Blood (Book 29)
Curtain Call (Book 30)

ONE

The way Dehan scratched her eyebrow said she was being patient.

"One of our criteria for picking a case is that it should be capable of being solved." She had her boots crossed on the corner of the desk, and I was leafing through what little there was of the file.

I said, "Yes."

The sigh was a small one that wanted to be a big one.

"This case is not capable of being solved, Stone. There is no evidence."

I considered the photograph of the young woman lying on her blood-soaked bed. It was a nauseating sight. I gave my head a couple of shakes. "That no evidence was found does not mean that there isn't any."

"Oh." Her voice was flat. "What does it mean?"

I raised an eyebrow at her over the file. "That none was found, Dehan."

This time, her sigh was more fulfilled. "Okay, talk me through and tell me where you think more evidence might be found."

I took my time staring out the window at a sagging, wet sky that was various shades of gray, none of them very interesting. My mind wandered a little to the half-naked branches of the plane trees across the road. They were patchy, silver and green, and below them a clutch of damp cops stood on the wet blacktop. They were in shirtsleeves. It was wet but not cold enough for jackets and coats.

"Autumn in New York," I said. She arched her eyebrows and did a bad job of concealing a smile. "Why does it seem so inviting? Sally Jones, twenty-two, lived at 1114 Commonwealth Avenue, in the top-floor apartment. She worked as a waitress at the Waddling Duck, a late-night bar on Westchester Avenue, between Beach and Taylor, opposite the dance school..."

"I know it."

"So, at about two thirty on the night of Tuesday the twelfth, early hours of Wednesday the thirteenth of October 2010, Sally closes up the bar at about one a.m. and heads for home. Midweek early closing."

"She was at the bar alone?"

I shook my head. "Nope. She was with Mary O'Brien, her work friend. According to the branch manager, Sally was very capable, and they had been giving her more responsibility. She was pretty, fun, lively, and good for business—and responsible with it. So, Mary's boyfriend collected her and took her home, and Sally walked the ten or fifteen minutes to her apartment."

"She made it home."

"It would seem so. It was a cold night—I checked—her coat was on the back of a chair in the living room–cum–dining room, there was a glass in the sink which contained traces of orange juice, apparently poured from a carton in the fridge, her shoes were beside her bed, her clothes were neatly folded on a chair, and she was dead in bed. According to Frank, who was the ME for this case, she never even woke up. She died in her sleep."

"Entry?"

I wagged a finger at her. "Interesting feature. The downstairs lock is electronic. You buzz the apartment and they press an electronic key on the entry phone. Standard. This had been overridden with some kind of device that triggered the opening mechanism."

"Huh, a techie."

"Perhaps. But the lock upstairs had simply been picked."

"CCTV cameras?"

"None upstairs, only in the front and back yards."

"So he knew."

"Perhaps he—or she—did. What we know as fact is that he picked the lock very expertly, and it would seem quietly, made it to the bedroom without knocking over any lamps."

"So either he had night-vision goggles or he knew the layout."

"It would seem so. Then, once beside her bed, he stabbed her violently in the heart. She died from this wound and—this is important—hemorrhaged profusely internally."

"He left the knife in until her heart had stopped pumping."

"Precisely. Our killer is cool and methodical. Then, once her heart had stopped pumping, he removed the knife and went into a frenzy."

"That way, he avoided getting covered in blood-spurt but vented some kind of rage against her. What kind of knife?"

"A large hunting knife with a serrated back. Now, there are three more points of interest: one, he or she removed Sally's hands. The cuts through the wrist were not expert—not a surgeon or a butcher—but there was a certain amount of skill involved. Two, her feet were removed in the same manner. Three, there was no sexual assault."

She stared at me for a long moment, and I stared back. It was a habit we had developed over time that made other people uncomfortable, but it helped us to think. Finally, she said, "There are ritualistic elements, like the removing of the hands and feet, suggestive of fetishism and keeping trophies, that one would normally associate with a serial killer or a killing where some kind of sexual fixation is involved. But she was not sexually assaulted, and there have been no reports of similar murders in New York State in the last nine years."

I nodded. "I've alerted the Feds officially that we are taking another look and are considering the serial killer angle, and I have spoken unofficially to Bernie at the bureau. So far, nothing has popped up with the same MO."

"You've done that already, without telling me."

"Yesterday, you were busy scowling at the clouds in the backyard. Moving on, there was zero forensic evidence, which speaks again to a very careful, methodical person. Conversations with her boss and Mary O'Brien, her work friend, threw up nothing. The team at the time interviewed several of the customers at the bar who were more friendly with her; none of them were able to provide any useful leads."

She shook her head. "No recent altercations, scenes, guys getting intense..."

I shrugged. "Presumably those were the standard questions that were asked, but nothing came up that was interesting enough to bring anybody in for a formal interview. What statements there are, are here." I waved the file at her. "But nobody mentions anything out of the ordinary."

She spread her hands, shrugged, and raised her eyebrows the way only people with Latin blood know how. "So you want to tell me how and where you think you're going to find more evidence?"

I took a deep breath and looked out at the sagging clouds, like wet laundry after a storm. Not much had changed. I shrugged, but without the Latin panache. "Sometimes, you just have to know how to ask a question."

"Right..." She frowned.

"And, more important, how to listen to the answer."

"And you think the investigating detective didn't know how to ask or listen."

"I don't know. Let's find out."

She looked at her watch. "Okay, Sherlock. The chief's press conference is up, let's go."

The press conference wasn't as grand as the name suggested. It was held in the briefing room with a few journalists from Bronx papers, a junior reporter from the *New York Times*, and one television crew from a right-wing TV network. Recently promoted Inspector John Newman, the station chief, was giving a brief talk to introduce us.

". . . the couple of years that this program has been running, Detectives Stone and Dehan have produced a string of over twenty convictions and brought closure to many families and loved ones. In addition, on occasions, we have been able to assist other PDs in closing cases that had gone cold within their own jurisdictions. The Forty-Third is proud of the success of this outstanding department." He turned to me and extended his hand. "John, would you care to come and answer a few questions?"

I frowned, glanced at Dehan, and stepped up to the lectern and the mics.

"Good morning." I pointed to Johnny Robles, a guy who had put more leads my way than any narc I ever ran. "Johnny."

"Detective Stone, you've cracked more than twenty cold cases since you started this department, and prior to that, you had the best arrest and conviction record in the Forty-Third . . ."

"Thanks for the plug, Johnny, what's your question?"

There was scattered laughter. He gave me a wink and went on, "I was hoping to be a producer on your upcoming reality show. But my question is, can you tell us about your current case?"

I glanced at the inspector, and he gave me a brief nod. I said, "As you know, I can't comment on an ongoing investigation, but I can tell you what is already in the public domain. On the tenth of October 2010, Sally Jones was murdered in her apartment here in the Bronx. It was a particularly violent, brutal killing, suggestive of intense rage, but the investigation at the time failed to turn up any witnesses, any suspects, or any motive."

The *New York Times* guy raised his hand, and I nodded at him. "How do you expect to unearth evidence capable of closing this case, ten years after the crime, when the investigating detectives at the time were unable to do so? Does this mean you have a license to cut corners? Or use strong-arm methods frowned on in modern police work?"

I raised two fingers in the V sign. "That's two questions. I can count. And I am pretty sure that was two." More scattered laughter. "Taking your questions in reverse order: no. And because my partner, Detective Dehan, and I are damned good at what we do."

The laughter was less scattered this time, and a few cops who'd poked their noses in the door laughed and clapped. *New York Times* wasn't all that popular at the 43rd. I pointed to the TV camera.

"Your work is dangerous, and I think it is fair to say you are on the front line twenty-four seven, Detective Stone. Yet your partner is also your wife. Can you tell us what that's like, and is it even allowed?"

I smiled. "Again, two. Detective Carmen Dehan is the best partner I have had in nearly three decades on the force. I am privileged to work with such a talented, skilled, and outstanding detective. As to commenting on my personal life and feelings, they are strictly out of bounds."

The camera had panned right to take her in, where she was leaning against the wall with her arms crossed. She raised an eyebrow at me but other than that showed no signs of being aware of the attention.

The questions went on for another five minutes, then Inspector John Newman called an end to the conference, and we made our way back toward our desks. The inspector caught up with us by the coffee machine, hurrying on worried legs.

"John! John, hold up a moment, will you?"

We stopped and turned to face him. He ran a couple of steps and came to a halt in front of us, nodding and looking at the gray carpeted floor.

"Excellent. Superb, both of you. Wonderful."

"Nothing to it, sir, just answering questions."

He nodded a lot. "No, no, yes, absolutely, look, thing is . . . um . . ."

"Is there a problem?"

"Thing is . . ." He glanced at Dehan a couple of times. "They loved you, Carmen, went down a bomb. Superb."

I frowned. "Are you planning to give Dehan a reality show, sir?"

He laughed too much, too loud, and too long. "No, no, Carmen is far too valuable as part of our team. But I know the way these things work, and the husband-and-wife cold-case team could very easily make national news. You saw the *New York Times* boy trying to raise the specter of improper practices. He could smell the chance of a scoop with nationwide interest."

Dehan had her eyes and nose screwed up. Oddly, it made her more beautiful. "What are you driving at, sir?"

"The case you've chosen."

I shook my head. "What about it?"

"It's notorious. It's referred to in criminology papers. It is an insoluble case, the perfect example of a perfect homicide."

I made a question with my eyebrows and asked it.

He sighed. "You will be the object of national scrutiny. The whole point of this conference was to showcase the cold-case department and its uninterrupted run of twenty successful investigations . . ."

Dehan snorted. "And you're worried the one case when the whole country is looking will be the one we can't crack."

His face folded into a rictus of embarrassed agreement.

I grunted and looked at my shoes. "Sir, I have already stated which case we are going to look at next. If we change that case now, the *New York Times* will be all over it like flies."

He stifled a sigh. "Yes, I know." His mouth started to form several questions, but he settled on, "You chose this case, why . . . ?"

I wasn't sure how to answer him, but Dehan narrowed her

eyes to a dangerous point and gave the answer I wished I had given. "Because it's a cold case, sir."

He nodded and looked at the carpet between his feet. "Always," he said, "so incisive and to the point."

He climbed the stairs and made for his office, a good man bending under the growing weight of politics.

Back at our desks, Dehan dropped into her chair, picked up a pencil, and held it between her two hands while she watched me. I remained standing and picked up the rather sparse file.

She said, "So, cited in papers on criminology as the classic insoluble case."

I nodded.

She narrowed her eyes. "You didn't know that before you chose it."

I screwed up my face and blew through my teeth. That was the best she was going to get by way of an answer, but she was no quitter.

"And you picked this case after the chief told you about the press conference."

I twisted my face into another "maybe, I don't remember exactly" face.

"You are one hell of an SOB, John Stone." I made a reluctant acquiescence face, and she grinned. "Guess that's why I can't resist you, you bad, bad man."

I suppressed a chuckle, which came out as a grunt. "Let us not get sidetracked by your erotic proclivities, Detective Dehan. We need to decide where to take a hold of this case. My own feeling is that we should start at the bar where she used to work and see if we can't track down some of the people she used to work with."

I was vaguely aware of Mo at the next desk across the aisle. He was with his new partner, Ivan Kawalski. Ivan had been reading the same piece of paper for the last ten minutes, and I figured he was asleep. Mo had been tapping at his computer but kept running his fingers through his hair. I smiled at Dehan and she smiled back.

She said, "Erotic proclivities? What does that mean?"

"Look it up."

She turned to Mo and spoke in a husky drawl. "Hey, Mo, can you tell me what an erotic proclivity is?"

"Aw, go to hell, the pair of you! Jesus, let a guy woik once in a while, wouldya!"

I shook my head. "He doesn't know either. C'mon. Get your jacket, we'll get lunch on the way."

TWO

We approached Westchester Avenue along Beach Street. The Bronx has a bad reputation. Let's be honest, it has a bad reputation to the point where it is an international icon for violence and racial unrest. The truth, almost twenty years into the twenty-first century, is a little different. But there are areas, and Westchester and Beach, and the streets in the general area, still have a flavor of the old Bronx. It's not exactly a concrete jungle—at least not during the day—but perhaps something of a rainforest: colorful, gaudy, noisy, and with plenty of hidden menace.

The buildings were one and two stories, the walls were old, weathered red brick, and the shop fronts were plastic and too shiny: convenience stores with absurdly exotic names like the Taj Mahal or the Star of Bombay; hair and nail stylists defying the doctrine of transgender and proclaiming themselves to be unisex. And the graffiti was everywhere, no longer defying the State and the status quo, but glorying in its own, bulbous illegibility: the drones from the Hive Mind, asserting their collective individuality.

The Waddling Duck was still there, on Westchester Avenue. The steel blind was down and covered in fat yellow and green letters that spelled no recognizable English words. There were bills too, advertising yoga classes, reggae workshops, Buddhist retreats, and Christian brotherhoods, alongside LGBT clubs with live music and talks on "Islam, a Religion of Peace and Love for the Future."

I double-parked my old burgundy Jaguar Mark II, put my hazards on, and we climbed out. Dehan stood examining the bills on the blind. I figured she was looking for something about closing and maybe reopening. I went to the unisex beauty salon next door. It was brightly lit and busy, with most of the chairs occupied by women having their hair permed by men.

A person who looked like he or she had been locked in his or her grandmother's cellar for the last twenty years, without food or light, approached me on legs taken on loan from a large spider.

"I'm Adrian? I'll be your beauty guide today? What was it you had in mind . . . ?"

Adrian allowed his eye to rove my unbeautiful body while he made a disapproving face. I took out my badge and showed it to him.

"No, you won't. What I want is information," I told him. "How long has the Waddling Duck been closed?"

"Oh, Lord . . ." It wasn't clear whether his dismay was at my being a cop, or the complexity of the question.

Dehan came in and stood beside me. She showed him her badge. "Detective Dehan."

He said again, "Oh, Lord!" But this time, the meaning was clear. "You're a cop? My dear, you should be a model! Never mind your skin, we can fix that, but those legs! They go on forever!"

"Thanks. I'll think about it. How long's the Duck been closed?"

"So . . ." He cupped his right elbow in his left hand and looked at Dehan along his eyes. "Two years? Lou died. Massive heart attack. He was such a big man with a vast appetite. His poor heart just couldn't take it. I know how it felt, believe me!"

I stopped him before he got into his mince. "Who's Lou?"

"Why, the owner! Lou was the Waddling Duck. Who else would come up with a name like that?"

Dehan looked at me with a face that was devoid of expression the way deep space is devoid of light. "Yeah, Stone, who else?"

I ignored her. "So you knew him well?"

"In the Biblical sense?"

"In any sense. Did you know him well?"

A shrill voice came to us from the back of the shop. "Ade? Are those people going to have their hair done or are you going to stand there talking all morning?"

The voice came from a portly Latino man in his late forties wearing the same black T-shirt and jeans as Adrian. Adrian made an elaborate job of tucking his chin into his neck and scowling at that man.

"Keep your long johns on, Cruella, it's the police asking about poor old Lou." He turned his attention back to me and raised an eyebrow. "Why are you asking about poor old Lou?"

The man he'd called Cruella approached on strutting legs, echoing Adrian as he came. "Lou is dead. He's been dead two years now. Why do you want to know about Lou?"

Dehan said, "We don't. We want to know about Sally Jones and her friends."

Cruella closed his eyes and plastered his left hand on his cheek.

Adrian dropped his jaw so far I could almost see Australia. "Oh," he said, "my . . . God! I cannot believe it!"

Cruella said, "That bitch!"

"Can you believe that bitch?"

"I can't believe it."

"What has she done?"

Dehan's voice was flat the way last night's beer is flat. "She's dead."

Cruella sounded affronted. "She was murdered!"

Adrian went with, "Well, we knew that!"

I said, "You knew that?"

"Everybody knew that. I don't think many people were surprised! If anybody had it coming, that minx did. It was the talk of the borough. Wasn't it, darling?"

This last was directed at Cruella, who shook his head like he was going to deny it, but said, "Everybody was talking about it."

I nodded. "So aside from the fact that she was a minx and a bitch, what else can you tell us about her? Who were her friends, and what was it, exactly, that made her a minx and a bitch?"

Adrian cupped his right elbow in his left hand again, cocked his hip, and stared at Cruella. "What made her a bitch?"

Cruella shook his head. "Any number of things. How about the way she would lead nice guys on, outrageous innuendos about what she would do with—or to—them. Winks, blowing them flirty kisses, showing her cleavage . . ."

Adrian cut in, "She had the most gorgeous cleavage. To die for!"

"And always on display. I mean . . ." He spread his arms like a black-and-white minstrel. "On permanent display at the Metropolitan Museum of Art! Sally Jones' cleavage!"

A few of the customers looked over and laughed. Adrian looked out the window and muttered, "Darling, a little outré . . ."

"I can't help it. She was so vulgar. And of course men . . . forgive me, Detective, but when it comes to women"—he eyed Dehan briefly—"all your taste is in your balls, and as for your brains, once you see a nice pair of legs or a buxom pair of boobs, you're about as smart as wearing high heels and a tight red dress to run the bulls in Spain . . ."

Adrian sighed noisily. "So outré . . . as I was saying. She was a tart and a hussy. If it was in pants, she'd ride it. If it had a fancy Porsche or Ferrari key ring, then you couldn't pry her off with a crowbar."

Dehan grunted. "What about her friends? She buddy up with the staff?"

Adrian shrugged. "She was tight with Lou. I mean, she attracted a lot of customers, so why should he care if she was a hussy or not? And Maya, the other full-time waitress. They were always hanging out. You'd think they'd get enough of each other at work, but apparently they liked each other." He gave Cruella a meaningful look that was on the bitter side of resentful.

I said, "Any idea where we can find this Maya? Surname, address . . . ?"

Cruella nodded. "Oh, sure. She's local." He turned into the shop and yelled, "Anyone know where that hussy Maya Hernandez lives?"

There were a couple of shouts of "Thieriot Avenue!"

But one woman was flapping her hand up and down like she knew something the others didn't. "No, no! She won't be home now. She's workin', doing waitressin' at Bill's Meat Emporium, just one block east. She in trouble?"

I thanked them, and we stepped out into the midday chill, where drizzle was threatening under a bellying gray sky. I climbed in behind the wheel, the doors slammed, and a small chill ran up my ankle. I fired up the old growler and rolled a hundred yards down the road to park outside a vast, brown building with plate glass doors and windows and the name BILL'S MEAT EMPORIUM emblazoned across the front in large, chrome letters. The lunch-hour rush hadn't started yet, and I found a space right outside. I parked and killed the engine, but Dehan remained immobile, frowning at the walnut dash.

"A tart and a hussy who'd ride anything in pants."

"An opinion, and not a very reliable one."

She shifted her frown to me. "But interesting in the context of an apparently motiveless killing."

I shrugged with my eyebrows. "I can't argue with that."

I climbed out, and she followed. A chill wind gusted down Westchester Avenue and whipped her hair across her face, so she had to finger it away as we pushed through the doors.

Inside, it was plush and quiet, carpeted in a thick, dark brown fabric that reached into every corner. Pale wood booths, upholstered in red imitation leather, lined the walls, while the center of the floor was occupied by round tables with white linen tablecloths. Directly in front of us, there was a lectern, and beside that a man with shiny black hair and a burgundy tuxedo that made him look oddly villainous.

"I am Bill," he announced, as though announcing a popular movement against Islamic fundamentalism, "and I would like to take a personal interest in making your dining experience something special for you to remember today. Table for two?"

I smiled at him without much feeling. "No, we are detectives with the NYPD, and we would like to speak to Maya Hernandez."

His eyes went circular, and his pupils became pinpricks, which he turned on our badges. "What has she done?"

"Nothing we are aware of. She was friends with the victim of a crime. We need to ask her some questions. Have you somewhere quiet we can talk to her?"

"In the kitchen!"

He balled his fists and swung them in front of him as he marched us to the kitchen and pushed through the swinging doors. The kitchen was large and all gleaming steel and white tiles. There were several people in white uniforms and four girls to one side working at a trolley of cutlery and crockery.

Bill bellowed, "Maya! Here, please!"

Maya Hernandez was not what I had expected. She was in her early thirties but looked younger. She had intense red hair tied back in a ponytail, a spray of freckles over very white skin, and translucent, deep green eyes. She hurried over with a small frown between her eyes, examining me and Dehan like she was looking for signs of danger.

"Yes, Mr. Brown."

"These are police officers . . ." He paused, staring hard into her face.

She glanced at us again and back at him. "Yes, Mr. Brown . . ."

I was growing tired of the guy, so I sighed loudly and cut in, "Ms. Hernandez, we won't take up much of your time. We just need to ask you some questions about Sally Jones." I turned to Bill. "Thanks, Bill. We'll let you know if we need anything."

He marched away with his fists hauling his disarranged dignity about him, and Maya led us to a small annex with an old sofa and a couple of threadbare chairs arranged around a polished pine and glass coffee table that had probably seemed like a good idea back when people thought mullets and sideburns looked cool. She sat on the sofa.

"This is where we take our breaks, if we get to take them."

We sat and showed her our badges.

She glanced at them. "What do you want to know about Sally? She died nine years ago."

Dehan answered. "We run a cold-case unit at the Forty-Third Precinct. Sally's case was never closed, so we want to take another look at it, see if something shows up this time that didn't show up before..."

She gave a small nod. "My roommate called. She saw you on TV. She said you were opening the case again."

"Like I said, it was never really closed. You were pretty close with Sally..."

"She was my best friend. Not everybody understood her, but I did." She smiled at the memories she was running through her head. "She was pretty wild, but she knew where to draw the line. It made a lot of guys mad, because they thought she was giving them the come-on, but she wasn't. She was just real friendly, and she had a naughty sense of humor. I still miss her."

"Forgive me for being blunt," I cut in, "but we need to be very clear about this. As I understand it, you are saying that Sally was very flirtatious and often gave men the wrong impression, that she was giving them the come-on."

She looked unhappy at the way I'd put it, but shrugged. "I guess you could put it that way."

"But she rarely followed through. So there might have been quite a lot of men, frequenting the Waddling Duck, who felt a bit sore and frustrated at having been led on and then dropped."

She sighed. "Well, that is the popular theory about what happened. And it is true that she was real popular with the guys. Business dropped big-time after she died. The guys used to go there to see her. She was like a celebrity. It wasn't just that she looked good, but her personality was huge. She was fun, funny, lively, always happy and bright . . ." She paused, sighed again, and shook her head at the coffee table. "And to be honest, most of the guys, once they realized she was just messing, took it well and were happy to be just flirty friends. I never saw anyone take it bad."

Dehan asked bluntly, "So was she promiscuous?"

Maya's eyes formed two big circles. "Heavens no! She never went home with any guys . . ." She stopped, raised her hands, and let them drop into her lap. "That's not strictly true. There was one guy—actually, there were a few that she kind of got close with, a handful, but this one in particular she really liked. He was very persistent, and persistence went a long way with Sally. He was big, very tough, a martial arts teacher. He didn't like her working at the bar, he didn't like the way she flirted, and he didn't like all the guys hanging around her. I think they broke up shortly before she died."

"How sore was he?"

She shook her head. "I don't know. We were close in many ways, but she really didn't talk about her private life much. She told me she was getting tired of him pressuring her and making demands, but that was about it."

I leaned forward with my elbows on my knees. "Maya, this could be real important. Can you remember this guy's name?"

She nodded and stared up at the ceiling. "Ben, he was always talking about his club, and the club was Ben's Mixed Martial Arts. I don't know if it's still going, but maybe you can find him on Google."

Dehan made a note of the name on her cell. "Was there anybody else, Maya? Anyone else she was close to? Anyone who seemed a bit obsessed or fixated, was trying to get close . . . ?"

"That's what they asked me at the time, and I think about it most weeks, but there really was nobody out of the ordinary. She was friendly with a lot of customers, but she wasn't close to anyone except Ben, and me."

"Among the people she was friendly with, does anyone stand out?"

"Not really, no. There were a couple of guys who used to chat to her at the bar some nights. She seemed to be fond of them, but they weren't close. One of them was a big, hairy guy. I think he was a mechanic. Gus. And the other guy was a bit of a nerd, lots of money. I think that was the main reason she hung out with him!" She laughed a pretty laugh. "But he kind of faded out after a while. Neither of them was real keen at all. Not like Ben."

Bill appeared at the door and scowled at us. "Are you done? I don't pay my staff to be informants for the police, Detectives. If you want to extend this interview, I am afraid it will have to be on her time, not mine!"

I glanced at Dehan.

She shrugged.

"We're done."

We thanked them both and stepped out onto the blustery sidewalk. There was a hint of blue peering between shaving cream clouds in the west, but in the east, they were as heavy and sodden with rain as they had been that morning.

Dehan stepped up close and looked into my face. "Emilio's Pizza, he'll have a fire burning today. I need a burger and a beer to start thinking this through."

I went around and opened the driver's door, speaking as I climbed in. "Already you're thinking it through?" I slammed the door. "That means you're being intuitive, and that never works. You know it."

She slammed her door too. "Shut up and drive me to my burger."

So I did.

THREE

In the car, headed back to the station house after a couple of burgers and a couple of beers, Dehan sat chewing on a toothpick and staring at the damp road ahead. It wasn't drizzling, but it was spitting and gearing up for rain that evening. I was listening to the pleasant hiss of the traffic on the wet blacktop as we moved down Morris Park Avenue. Dehan spoke suddenly.

"One of two scenarios: one, she came on a little too strong to the wrong guy, and when she tried to turn him down, he killed her. Two, she was into something which she was keeping real quiet, and it backfired."

I glanced at her and smiled. She didn't see it. I said, "Something like?"

"Drugs, prostitution . . . some kind of illegal service provided to dangerous people."

I sighed. "It's too soon, Dehan. We still know virtually nothing."

She wagged her left finger at me without averting her eyes from the road. "We know as much as the previous investigating detectives knew, and we are unlikely to learn more. If we want to crack this one, we'd better start formulating theories pronto. Because this case is back to front, Stone."

"What do you mean, it's back to front?"

"Usually, you follow the evidence and see where it leads you, then you formulate your theory. That's not going to work this time. We need to start formulating theories and let them lead us toward the evidence, if there is any."

I made a face that said she had made a good point and a surprising one.

"Okay, well, a sexually motivated murder is unlikely for the simple fact that she was not raped."

"Ah!" She turned in her seat to look at me. "But not if he was impotent."

I frowned. "Okay, explain that to me."

"Just theorizing for the sake of theorizing: let's assume the guy she is coming on to is shy, introverted, and timid, and that's why nobody noticed him. The reason he is shy and timid is because he is sexually impotent. Whatever his medical condition is, we don't know right now, but it's irrelevant, because what is important is that he can't perform."

"Okay."

"Now, maybe she finds him cute, or maybe she just comes on to everybody. Thing is, she comes on to him, and he believes it and starts to fantasize that maybe she can help him overcome his condition."

"That's a reach."

"No, it's a theory. Now, just when he is beginning to believe his fantasy, she lets him down. And here is the interesting part. The nature of the mutilation is consistent with classical Freudian castration fantasy. So, correct, we have zero evidence as a result of that theory, but we do have subtle pointers that we might be overlooking a shy, timid young man with severe emotional problems due to his sexual impotence. It is something to look for."

I nodded for a long while. "That's good. Yes, Dehan. That's good. What about theory number two?"

She spread her hands. "People kill primarily over intimate relationships. Husband, wife, lovers, children, and parents, and on the face of it, that does not seem to have been the case here. There has been no mention of a husband or any family member. The closest we've come is Ben the MMA teacher. Frankly, pure gut feeling, Stone, an MMA teacher is going to beat you to death with his fists or break your neck—especially if his motive is sexual jealousy. I don't see him stabbing you fifteen times and then cutting off your hands and feet."

"Let's reserve judgment on that."

"Fine. But if we are not talking about some kind of fetishism involving castration, I see this as a punishment killing. Mexican gangs go in for dismemberment big-time."

I screwed up my face. "Nyeah . . . That tends to be in Mexico, and as well as that, the body is usually displayed, hung from a bridge or from a lamppost, or scattered on the road. It isn't normally left in the apartment."

"Okay, I am just saying that as an alternative, for me, dismemberment usually would mean an emotionally disturbed killer taking a trophy or acting out a castration, or organized crime sending a message."

"Point taken." I turned south onto White Plains. "But I am finding it hard to imagine this girl being involved in any kind of organized crime without either her friend Maya knowing it or word reaching the dynamic duo, Adrian and Cruella De Vil, through the gossip telegraph network."

"Hmmm . . ." It was the sound of being unconvinced. "Unless it was some form of prostitution."

"When would she have time?"

She shook her head. "No, you don't get it. She's the agent, perfectly placed, turns on the guys, then tells them, 'Not me, pal, but I know a girl who will.'"

"That's actually feasible."

"Thanks."

I turned off White Plains and onto Story and a couple of minutes later pulled up outside the station house. Early afternoon, damp and clouded, felt like late afternoon, and for a moment I had a pang to be at home, lighting the fire and sipping a Martini while Dehan started dinner. It would rain tonight, and it would be a slow, damp crawl home through liquid light on the blacktop.

We climbed out, and the doors of the Jag made a damp echo as they closed. Dehan fell into step with me as we crossed toward the entrance.

"So, summing up your two theories," I said. "We might be looking for a shy, introverted guy who nobody notices and who is sexually impotent, or evidence that Sally was acting as an agent for prostitutes selling their services through the Waddling Duck."

"That could also account for the popularity of the place at the time, and the fact that its popularity waned so dramatically when she died."

I nodded as we pushed through into the detectives' room. "Okay, well, the most we can do is play with them at this stage. The next thing we need to do is track down Ben of the MMA and have a talk with him. We also need to start tracking down people who frequented the Duck back at that time, who remember Sally, and see if they can flesh out some of these people she used to hang with."

Dehan dropped into her chair and rolled over to her laptop, where she started rattling keys. I stood a moment, scratching the back of my neck and trying to visualize how Sally's putative prostitution agency would work. How, for example, would she protect the girls from abuse and violence?

That was when del Rio called to me from across the room.

"Hey! Stone! I got a case would interest you!"

I've never been popular or great at socializing with other cops, but I try to keep it cordial, so I smiled and said, "Yeah?"

"Sure." He came over and stood in front of me, with his knees jerking out to the sides and moving his neck like he was trying to adjust it into his collar. "Get this, right? 1965 Ford Mustang Fastback, in perfect condition, once owned by Steve McQueen three years before he made *Bullitt*. This babe is worth upward of five hundred grand and it was stolen from right under the owner's nose, from his country estate. You like classic cars, right? You got that sweet old Jag out there. I thought, Stone's gonna appreciate this one."

I nodded. "A '65 Mustang is a nice car. Pristine and once owned by Steve McQueen, no way that's going to fetch less than six hundred grand at auction. Maybe close to a million, depending who's at the sale."

"'Swat I thought."

Dehan had swiveled around in her chair and was staring at the back of del Rio's neck. "You're telling me the guy stole a '65 Mustang Fastback from a country estate and nobody noticed?"

Del Rio turned and eyed Dehan with caution. "Ain't that a thing? There's like fifty acres of land. Guy's got a river, forest, hills. His nearest neighbor is, like, over a mile away. So the place is quiet like the grave. Somehow this guy—I figure he's like the Saint, you know? Somehow he gets in, makes it to the house without being seen or heard, breaks into the exhibition room..."

Dehan cut him short. "An exhibition room?"

"Yeah, the guy is a multimillionaire collector of classic cars. That's why I figured Stone would be interested, right? So this guy breaks into the exhibition room, takes the damn car, and drives it away without nobody noticing."

Dehan shook her head. "It's not possible."

"Whadd'ya talkin' about? The car is gone. I been there. I seen it!"

Dehan flapped a hand at him. "He's playing you, del Rio! He's going to claim on the insurance and sell the car to some Russian on the black market!"

"Yeah? You think I didn't think of that?" He turned to me. "Your wife. She give you a hard time like this too?" He turned back to her. She was typing again. "First damn thing I thought of! So I checked every barn, every stable, every copse, every inch of woodland. I got the damned chopper to fly over."

She didn't even look at him. "It was never there."

"Not there, huh? So how come every single member of staff, twenty people altogether, swear they saw it arrive and they saw it displayed in the showroom. How come, smarty-pants, he showed me the documents that prove the transport company delivered the damn car there four weeks ago? How come he gave me the telephone number and address of the transport company so I could check it out?"

She sighed and flopped back in her chair. "The car was definitely delivered there because there are too many people involved for it to be a conspiracy."

He pointed at her. "That's my thinkin'."

"It was there for four weeks on display, and then vanished, when?"

"This morning, just before lunch. The guy who looks after the cars went to clean them and the darned Mustang was gone."

"None of the others?"

"Nope, only the Mustang."

"What about the alarm system?"

"I'm having it examined right now. But all the doors and windows are triple glazed, and once they are closed, you cannot hear a damned thing outside. What we got here is a damned sophisticated, high-class thief."

He slapped me on the shoulder. "You take it easy, pal. I'll see you around."

Dehan muttered, "Not if I see you first," but del Rio was gone and didn't hear her. I lowered myself into my chair, and she looked at me with those disturbingly direct eyes she had.

"What are you doing?"

I raised an eyebrow. "Gazing at the most beautiful thing in the galaxy and perhaps the universe. What are you doing?"

She wrinkled her nose and winked at me. "Benjamin Gaditano, American born of Cuban parents, professional cage fighter with a string of victories and championships, mostly knockouts. Doing well out of the Ben's Mixed Martial Arts Club, here in the Bronx, but currently at the East Coast MMA championships in

Philly. The championships last all week. So if we want to see him, we'll have to go to Philadelphia, to the cage fights."

"Is it too late to enter you? We could make some extra cash while we're there."

"You're funny."

"I know." I nodded. "Deep down funny."

"Where it's not like funny anymore."

"Good, so now we have dealt with that, why don't you book us into an hotel in Philly?"

Mo, who usually worked hard at studiously ignoring us, now turned to look at me in disgust. "'An hotel'? Seriously?"

"The 'h' is silent, Mo. A man of your breeding should know that."

Dehan snorted again as she booked our room. "Breeding? The only breeding Mo ever got was when his mother mistook him for one of her sow's litter of piglets and he spent a week in the sty being reared by Momma Pig. It was like Tarzan of the Apes, only it was Mo of the Swine."

There was reluctant laughter from the nearest desks. Somebody shouted, "She got you again, Mo!" Mo grumbled something, and we grabbed our jackets and made our way out to the car again. I threw her the keys, and she climbed behind the wheel. She turned the key in the ignition, and the old engine growled into life.

As we pulled out of the lot, I asked her, "So, following your strategy, what are we looking for in Ben?"

She shook her head and made for the Bronx River Parkway. "No, the strategy is the same, Stone. We follow the evidence and see where it takes us. But there is a strategy B if we find there is no evidence leading us anywhere . . ." She nodded a few times as we accelerated north. "It's heretical." She glanced at me. "It goes against all investigative dogma. But what we do is we develop loose, flexible theories based on what information we have, and then we say, 'If this is true, then this evidence should be there.' If she was killed by organized crime because she was running a prostitution network that trod on their toes, then there should be prostitutes out there who worked with her, there must be punters who she sent to them . . ."

"So, following that loose, flexible theory, we need to interview Ben with these scenarios in mind, and he might give us some information that points to either one or another of them."

"Theoretically," she said, and grinned.

I scratched my head. "But there could be a thousand of these possible theories."

"Not really, Stone. Once you start working through them, anything beyond organized crime or sexual motivation starts to become farfetched."

"What about family?"

She shrugged. "Like what?"

"Like a father or a mother who is so outraged at the life she is leading that they kill her."

She looked at me and screwed up her nose. "And cut off her hands and feet?"

I made a "hmmm" noise that said I agreed. "Problem is," I added, "killing someone and then cutting off their hands and feet is farfetched, so the explanation is, by definition, going to be farfetched."

"I agree, Stone, but of those farfetched explanations, organized crime and an obsession with castration are the least farfetched."

I studied her profile for a long while as she drove and smiled privately to herself. Finally, I said, "Am I playing catch-up here?"

Her smile became a grin. "I think you might be, big guy. I think you might be."

"Well, goddarn!"

We drove in silence for a bit while I turned her theories over in my mind and tried to think of others.

Eventually, she sucked her teeth noisily and said, "What about that Mustang, huh?"

"What about it? I was never crazy about muscle cars."

"I love them. Especially the early Mustangs. Hell of a ride in a straight line."

"They made up in brute force what they lacked in style and handling."

"Exactly, a bit like you."

"Thanks."

"But, Stone, what I was really getting at was the theft. That was one hell of a job!"

I eyed her for a moment. "We're homicide, Dehan. And cold cases, at that."

She nodded a few times, pursing her lips. "I know. Just sayin', one hell of a job to pull off."

Then she grinned at me and winked.

FOUR

The venue for the East Coast MMA championships was an abandoned warehouse on East Tioga Street, in a dilapidated industrial estate that had long since lost its industry. It was conveniently located just south of the I-95 and a few blocks west of the Betsy Ross Bridge.

The building was a long, concrete nave, three stories high and painted an unpleasant beige that was now peeling in gray patches. The roof was gabled, and most of the back wall above fifteen feet was composed of windows made of small glass panes contained in peeling iron frames that had once been painted red. It was Victorian in feel, though it probably dated to the '50s.

Out front, there was a large, dirt parking lot. There was only a handful of cars, so we parked by a Ford truck near the entrance, killed the engine, and stepped out onto damp, compacted earth pockmarked with puddles. It was midafternoon. I saw Dehan shudder and stand scanning the area. It was more like a nature reserve than an industrial estate.

"Every one of them closed down," she said. "Every one of them reclaimed by trees, weeds, birds, and bees."

I nodded. "Temporarily. Before long, they'll be converted into small, luxury apartments for executives working for foreign corporations building industrial estates in Third-World countries, where labor and land are cheap. And the cycle goes on."

She nodded. "Exploitation. It's what we do. Everybody is exploiting someone."

I held out my arm. "Come on, Professor Marx, our comrades await us."

She gave me a playful punch to the shoulder, which hurt, and called me a dumbass. Then we stepped in through the huge door of the building. It was hard to tell at first glance whether it had been a factory or a warehouse. The whole thing had been gutted, aside from a small office at the far right, so that now it was more like a cathedral, a place of worship, than a place of work.

There were people scattered here and there, some sparring, others training on their own, yet others in small groups, practicing moves. Their voices, shouts, and barked orders echoed high above our heads in the dark, cavernous ceiling. And occasionally there was the loud report, like a gunshot, of a fist or a foot smacking into a sack, or a body hitting the tatami.

The vast floor space had been divided into working areas, but at the center, like a sacred altar, was what it all revolved around: a huge cage, the octagon, thirty feet across and six feet high. Right then, it was empty, but beyond it, there was a tatami of similar proportions, without walls, where a bunch of guys were sitting, watching two other guys beat the hell out of each other. Dehan pointed, and we made our way toward them.

There was a guy in bare feet, black jeans, and a black T-shirt sitting on the far side of the tatami. He saw us approaching and stood. He walked around the sitting group and came to meet us at the octagon. He had the kind of face you could break your fist on. He was about six-one and solid muscle. He didn't smile. He challenged courteously instead.

"Afternoon. What can I do for you guys?"

I smiled. "Good afternoon. We're looking for Benjamin Gaditano."

"Is that so? Who's we?"

I showed him my badge. "This is Detective Dehan, I am Detective John Stone. We're with the NYPD. We'd like to ask Mr. Gaditano a few questions."

"You're a little out of your jurisdiction, aren't you?"

I offered him a small smile and a small shrug to go with it. "Unless you're Mr. Gaditano, then that's none of your business."

His face flushed, and his breathing quickened slightly.

I watched him with interest for a moment, then said, "If you're not Mr. Gaditano, can you either point him out or let him know we're here?"

"I'm Ben Gaditano, what do you want?"

I heard Dehan sigh. "Mr. Gaditano, if this is inconvenient for you, we can go 'round to your club in the Bronx. Then we'll be within our jurisdiction and that will make things easier. Right now, all we want to do is ask you some questions."

The threat was clear, and he closed his eyes a moment before answering. "Questions about what?"

I said, "We run a cold-case unit at the Forty-Third Precinct. We're looking at Sally Jones' case. We understand you were pretty close to her at one time."

He shrugged. "Sure I was. That's no secret. You guys asked me a bunch of questions when she was killed. I told you everything I knew back then."

I nodded. "Like I said, Mr. Gaditano, we are taking another look at the case, and we would appreciate your help."

At the back of the room, there was a loud yell and a loud smack as somebody hit the floor. It echoed in the rafters, and Ben glanced over. He gave a private smile, then shrugged. "Fine. Shoot. What do you want to know?"

"How serious was your relationship?"

The answer came back quick as a flash. "For her or for me?"

Dehan answered. "How about both?"

He leaned his back against the octagon and crossed his arms. "For me, it was pretty serious. I was thinking of making her my wife, kids, making a home. I told her. I don't mess around. Look around you. This is all me. I'm driving this thing. I say I'm gonna do something, you better believe I'm gonna do it. I told her, 'We gonna be married, baby. You're gonna be Mrs. Gaditano, and you are gonna have five little Gaditanos keepin' you busy every day while I build the greatest MMA fighting club in history.'"

Dehan cut in, "How'd she feel about that?"

He screwed up his face like she'd asked him his one times table. "Well, that's kind of my point, right? She told me it was a dream come true. She led me along, like I was her goddamn hero, the man of her dreams . . ." He did a bad imitation of a woman's voice. "'Oh, Ben, you're so big and strong, sweep me off my feet!' But when I told her to pack in her job, she told me no way."

"So maybe she liked her job."

"That's the point, wiseass! Her job, if you can call it that, was flirting with guys till four in the morning and getting them to buy drinks. Now I'm gonna ask you a question. What kind of job is that for a decent girl? It's like one step up from whoring. Maybe not even that! I mean, how the hell do I know what else goes on? How the hell do I know what else she's doing? Who the hell she's going home with at four a.m.?"

I said, "Are you saying you think she was engaged in prostitution?"

"Whoring. I call it whoring, because that's what it is. And I'm telling you, I don't know. I'll tell you this, she was never short of cash. She was damn careful with it though. She never paid for a goddamn thing when she was with me, or if there was some other guy around who she could get to pay for it."

Dehan was frowning and scratched her head. "Explain something to me." She gestured around. "You spend a lot of time at the club . . . ?"

He gestured at her with an open hand and nodded, like she'd made a fair point. "I don't drink and I don't smoke. I met Sally because she started coming to my club to learn to fight. Then she told me I should come along one night and pick her up from work. She'd cook me breakfast." He gave a small, bitter laugh. "I thought it was just me, but I guess I was one of a long line of guys who got to have breakfast with her." He shrugged. "Anyhow, I didn't like her work or the place where she was working. I told her so, but she said she made a lot of money on tips and she couldn't afford to pack it in."

"So you started frequenting the club?"

He shrugged his huge shoulders. "Of course. That's my girl. I want to keep her safe, right? But the more time I'm there, the more I'm seeing how she's flirting with every guy who comes along. And I ain't just talkin' about batting her eyelashes. I'm talkin' about full-blown innuendo. You know, like, 'Oh, you're a plumber? You'll have to come and look at my tubes!'"

Dehan arched her eyebrows. "Ouch! She said that in front of you?"

"I got real mad at that one, but she said it was all part of an act and it didn't mean nothin'. I tried to make her understand it meant something to me, that my girl was talkin' like that to other guys. But she couldn't see that."

"So what happened?"

"Nothing happened. I finally realized I was being a sap and that she was nothing better than a cheap whore. So I dumped her."

I scratched my head and shook it at the same time. "There must have been one incident, the straw that broke the camel's back. Something that made you come to that realization."

He took a deep breath and puffed out his cheeks. "Not really. It was more like a drip drip. One night, it dawned on me that she hadn't spoken to me for over an hour, but she'd flirted with just about everybody at the bar. I left and I don't think she even noticed."

Dehan asked him, "How mad were you?"

The only way to describe the expression on his face was contempt. "You don't hurt a woman, even if she's a filthy, low-down whore."

I cut in. "We're almost done, Mr. Gaditano. I'd like to know a little about the other people that she was close to or friendly with."

"Sally?" He said it like he hadn't realized we were talking about her. "Sally wasn't even close to me. There was a waitress, some Irish or Scottish chick with a Hispanic name. They were pretty tight. Aside from that, there were a few guys she might talk to most nights, but that was only because they were there most nights. Sally, if you weren't there, right in front of her, she already forgot you existed."

"Any of those other guys spring to mind?"

He nodded. "There was some Ivy League guy. She said he was old money and wanted to string him along. And then there was some dude. He looked like a wannabe Angel. Denim, leathers, long hair, tattoos. You know the type. I think he stepped in where I stepped out. They weren't the kind of guys you'd expect to hang out together. But that was Sally. Guys would do anything to get in her pants, and then she'd walk away and forget them."

Dehan asked, "Names?"

He examined the floor for a bit, then looked up into the cavernous rafter, like the names might be written up there.

"I can't remember the Ivy League guy's name. It wasn't weird, but it wasn't normal, like Pete or Joe. It might have been Jewish. The biker was called Gus. She talked about him a lot, that's why I remember."

"You didn't mention him in your original statement."

He shrugged. "To be honest, by then, I guess it didn't seem important. I was pretty sure she'd been killed by some guy she'd stood up, and I didn't care. Kind of thing that happens to whores."

I nodded. "And that's who she was talking to the night you left."

It wasn't a question, but he nodded anyway, then added, "They were talking about how women liked a bit of rough play. She did. She liked to get smacked around a bit. Not my scene, but she enjoyed it. She was telling Gus that a little bit of pain was a turn-on."

"Any idea how we can get in touch with Gus?"

He shook his head and pulled the corners of his mouth down. "I know he had a motorcycle workshop. He used to customize bikes and the like."

Dehan snapped, "Where?"

"Right there, at the corner of Westchester and White Plains, behind the gas station."

"You ever go there? Try to have it out with Gus?" She gestured at him. "You'd probably take him easy."

He held her eye for a long moment. I was curious to see what he would say. "Detective, I'm good. I'm probably the best around at the moment. But this is an art, and I don't use it to even scores or humiliate people. I will defend myself from physical attack. But you know what I do when people come into my life and try to hurt me? I do Zen meditation, and I detach myself from the pain. That is my path."

I'd heard enough, and I glanced at Dehan. She shrugged and shook her head at me. "Thanks for talking to us, Mr. Gaditano . . ."

He interrupted me, frowning out at the damp, gray afternoon. "There was somebody," he said, "now that you mention it, who did go to talk to Gus. I heard it on the grapevine, can't remember from who. It may have been the waitress." He shook his head. "I may be getting confused here. I bumped into this chick after Sally had died. And she told me that Sally's brother had gone to talk to Gus. I didn't even know she had a brother. I guess that's why it stuck in my mind. But I wasn't real interested and I don't listen to gossip, so I moved on."

I frowned. "Did you retain anything at all about him, where he lives, his name . . . ?"

He shook his head again. "Nah, just that he was some kind of big shot. But I'm sorry, that's about it. And anyhow, I need to get back to my students." He pushed himself away from the wire wall of the cage and held Dehan's eye for a moment. "It ain't just fighting and beating the hell out of people. It's mental and emotional discipline as well, and respect for decent values. Maybe you should look into it."

She nodded. "I'll do that. Thanks for your time."

We stepped out into the damp late afternoon. Just inside the door, a disciple in black jeans and a black T-shirt was putting up a billboard with a picture of Ben on it. Beside him was another guy who looked like he'd been cast in reinforced concrete. Underneath their pictures, it said, THE FIGHT OF THE CENTURY, UNBEATEN KING BEN GADITANO DEFENDS HIS TITLE AGAINST IVAN THE TERRIBLE, THE UNDEFEATED COSSACK TERROR.

Dehan tossed me the keys, and I caught them left-handed. We climbed in and slammed the doors. Spots of rain started to accumulate on the windshield. I turned the key, and the engine roared. "It's not getting any clearer."

She glanced at me, and there was mischief in her smile. "You think not, Watson?"

I bumped and rolled toward the exit onto the blacktop. "Okay, I grant you, he did seem to suggest she was involved in prostitution, but I think his opinion was colored by jealousy and a deep feeling of rejection."

She nodded. The windshield wipers set up a slow squeak-thud rhythm. "You may be right. For my part, I am beginning to see some interesting features in the case."

I smiled at her as we pulled onto the blacktop. "I have never seen you smug before. I think I like it."

"Jerk."

FIVE

I was hunkered down in front of the fire, watching the flames lick around the coals. I picked up my Martini from the floor and took a sip. I thought about the flavor for a moment, watching the flames grow in strength, and said, "I think the brother is important."

I heard the fridge door open and then close with a muffled thud. "What makes you say that?"

A closed question instead of an open one. I knew she was teasing me because open questions were a pet gripe of mine. I stood and moved to the breakfast bar, where she was sprinkling coarse salt onto two bison steaks.

"We had discounted the family member scenario, because there was no mention in the original report of a family member. But now it emerges we not only have a family member, but it is a brother, capable of disturbed feelings of jealousy and possessiveness toward his sister. Much more to the point, though, is the very fact that no mention of a brother—or any family—was made in the original report. What set of circumstances leads a family to be so estranged that when the daughter or sister is murdered, the family either don't hear about it, or, if they do, they don't come forward?"

She nodded as she smeared sunflower oil on the griddle. "And the case made the national news. It would be really hard for them not to have heard about it."

"So the first order of business tomorrow is to track down Sally's brother, and any other family members, and find out what the deal was with that family."

She dropped the two steaks on the smoking griddle and pointed at me with her finger like a gun. "You do that, I want to go and find Gus and ask him about his relationship with Sally."

I was surprised, and my eyebrows said so. "Oh?"

"I agree, the whole issue with the brother is weird. And I agree we have to look into it. But my gut is telling me this is all about her night life, the way she played guys, the shift from Ben to Gus. I can't tell you what it is yet, but I have a hunch, Stone."

I took a handful of cutlery from the drawer, carried it to the table, and started setting two places.

"If you have a hunch, then we should play it. But it's going to take us no more than half an hour to get the background on her family. Wait for me and we'll go see Gus together."

She nodded as she flipped the steaks.

I laughed. "What's got into you? You've really got the bit between your teeth with this case."

She smiled at me, and her eyes were warm and close. "I don't know. I just have a feeling."

WHAT WE TURNED up on Sally's family was not what we had expected. We started with her Social Security number and, through that, got hold of her birth certificate and her parents' names. When we tracked them down, it turned out her mother had died when Sally was just four, her father was a decorated marine with the rank of major, and her brother, who was fifteen years older than her, was also a marine and had seen action in both the Iraq wars and in Afghanistan.

By that time, I had recruited the help of Sergeant Penelope Hernandez, who had a background in research, to look deeper while we examined what we had. Dehan was reading Major David Jones' curriculum and bouncing a pencil on the desk while I was looking at the war record of his son, Lieutenant Ewan Jones.

That was when Sergeant Hernandez came in, squinting at me. "I think you ought to see this right away, Detective." She handed me a few sheets of printed paper stapled together at the corner. "I noticed when I was getting their war records that both Lieutenant Jones and Major Jones belonged to the Sacred Brotherhood of Christ. The family is originally from Belfast, in Maine, where that sect originated. So I thought, for the sake of completeness, I should look it up." She gave her head a little shake. "It's not what you might expect."

"Oh." I glanced over at Dehan. She was frowning at me and at Hernandez by turns. "Thank you, Sergeant."

She grimaced and went away. I glanced through it, then raised my eyebrows high at Dehan and started to read aloud.

"The Sacred Brotherhood of Christ was constituted in 1649 by Brother Charles McDonnell, after having seen an image of Jesus Christ galloping along the shores of Belfast Bay, wielding a sword. Brother Charles had been fishing at the time in a small rowing boat. He hurried ashore, disembarked, and found himself face-to-face with the image of the Lord.

"Brother Charles described it as the most magnificent, terrifying sight he had ever beheld: 'Upon his brow he bore a golden crown, His armor was of gold, as was His mount, and flames of luminous blue flickered and flicked about Him, as though the very air burned in the power of His presence. In his left hand, he held the reins of his mighty steed, which reared and pawed the sandy shore. In his right, he held aloft a gleaming sword of gold and silver encrusted with gems, which seemed to me to be the very semblance of Excalibur itself. And though I knew in my heart that the Lord had rejected all trappings of wealth, luxury, and worldly power, yet so also did I know that these endowments he bore were not but outward expressions of his own glory, not accrued by pillage and plunder, but manifest of His most magnificent and godlike soul.

"'Therefore did I fall upon my knees and lay myself flat upon the sand in a fever of awe and agitation. And then did the Lord speak to me. And his voice was like an angelic alarum calling down from the heavens. "Brother Charles, lie not thee upon thine belly like a common Saracen, for thou art chosen of the Lord. Stand thee upon thine feet, for which purpose did the Lord grant them thee. Call thee thine brothers to arms, for hear me well, this be not a time of peace, but a time to seek out evil and destroy it with sword and fire where'er you do find it. Evil is abroad, in sorcery and witchcraft, in paganism and Satanic orgies of the flesh. The second millennium is upon us, and know thee that Satan walks among you, with gin and opium, selling the vile pleasure of the flesh, and upon each side does he bear tethered a whore of Babylon. Go forth, Brother Charles, and call your people to arms!"

"'And so saying, he reared up upon his mighty steed and galloped upon a golden path of flame, up into the heavens, leaving me quivering and quaking upon the sand. When finally I recovered myself sufficiently to stand, I hurried forth to speak with the mayor and the reverend...'"

I paused, scanning ahead. "Essentially, they formed the Brotherhood and spent the next few years terrorizing Waldo County, and a little farther afield, burning and putting to the sword anyone whom they believed to be a servant of the Devil." I drew breath and cleared my throat. "'In the tiny hamlet of Swanville did we find a married couple. He bore upon his back the cloven mark of the Devil's hoof, whereby before birth the Devil himself had chosen the poor wretch as his servant in the world. His wife, besotted and entranced by her husband, fell upon us, weeping and begging for his life, and then, moved by God and in hope of redemption, beseeched us spare his life if she confessed to witchery. This she did and wept and screamed most wretchedly when she was burned at the stake. It moved one's heart to compassion and pity to see such a thing. But the Lord's work must be done without compassion or pity, for these are proper to the Lord and not to Man. The boy was beheaded, disemboweled, and burned to ashes.'"

I skipped forward to the end of the article. "Today the Brotherhood has some two hundred members, more than it had in 1649! But today, instead of scouring Maine for transgressors of the Lord's Law, the Brothers organize charity events and raise funds for worthy causes, such as finding a cure for cancer and, this year's big drive, helping to save the children of drug traffickers and lead them to Jesus."

She dropped the pencil on the table and drummed a little tattoo with her fingertips. "How the hell was that missed in the original investigation?"

"That's a good question, but a more immediate one is, are we looking at a motive for murder?"

"It's possible, yeah." She shrugged. "Nobody else has mentioned him. Maya didn't even mention him to us. Her family was not present in her life, yet he shows up out of the blue to go and talk to Gus just before she dies. Even if the Brotherhood doesn't get up to that kind of activity anymore, if he holds those values close to his heart, Sally's behavior might just have sent him over the edge. Plus, he's seen death. He's probably killed . . ."

I grunted. "Killing an enemy in war is not the same as killing your sister for living an unchristian life . . ."

A flicker of irritation crossed her face. "I know that, Stone. But killing anyone at all is inconceivable for most people, yet that was a barrier he had presumably already crossed."

"We need to find out if he's still in the Corps and where he's living."

Dehan picked up the phone, and I went to get some coffee. When I got back, she was arguing on the phone.

"Listen, pal . . . Okay, listen, Lieutenant, I am not telling you you shouldn't deal with your own problems in-house. I am not even telling you you have a problem. I'm just asking you for Lieutenant Ewan Jones' contact details."

She listened, drumming the table, sighing, and staring at the ceiling. Finally, she said, "I know, I know, I know—you said that already. But this is a police investigation and we need . . . I know you take disciplinary action very seriously, and I am aware of your jurisdiction . . . !"

She stared at the receiver for a while with her eyebrows high on her forehead. Then she looked at me. "He hung up on me. He was like twenty, and he hung up on me. The creep!"

I handed her a cup of coffee. "The Corps are a closed shop. Let me see if I can cut corners through Bernie at the bureau."

I pulled my cell, and as I was dialing, the desk phone rang. Dehan snatched it and barked.

"Dehan." She stared at me blankly, then said, "Thanks, Maria, put him through." She jerked her head at the other receiver. "Captain Ewan Jones."

I picked it up and heard Maria saying, "Go ahead, Captain Jones."

"Good afternoon, with whom am I speaking?"

"This is Detective John Stone, Captain Jones. My partner, Detective Dehan, is also on the line. We were just trying to run down your contact details, Captain."

His voice was gravelly, like he had smoked too many cigarettes and drank too much whiskey in the past. "I know. I saw the news broadcast this morning and I have been wrestling with my conscience all day."

"Why's that, Captain?"

"Because my family disowned Sally a long time ago. I fully supported the decision at the time, and I still do. But as well as a servant of God, Detective, I am also an officer in the United States Marine Corps, and I have a duty to uphold the law of these federal states. So I have a duty to contact you and tell you what I know of her last days. Even though that means that our family is once again dragged into the miasma of corruption, filth, and debauchery that was my sister's life."

"We will try to be as discreet as we can, Captain, and keep your family out of it if it is at all possible. Captain, may I just ask you how it is that you are not mentioned in the report of the original investigation? You must have been aware of your sister's murder, and surely the investigating officers attempted to contact you . . . ?"

He was quiet for a moment. "My father prevailed upon friends. It had nothing to do with us—she had nothing to do with us—so we were not contacted or mentioned, just as the Robinsons at 22 Florence Drive were not contacted, or the Smiths at 44 Apple Orchard Drive were not notified."

Dehan shook her head and covered her eyes with her hand.

I went on, "But you have a different view now?"

"Somewhat."

"I believe you came to visit your sister shortly before she was killed."

"I did. She was working nights late at some swarming den of iniquity, serving drinks to men, fornicating with them . . . she was the incarnation of the whore of Babylon. I was ashamed. She was also hanging around in the company of some kind of Hells Angel."

"You went to see him."

"I did. But Detective Stone, would it not be better for us to meet in person?"

"It would. Where are you, Captain Jones?"

"I am in Belfast, in Maine. I will come to you. I'll drive down tonight and see you first thing in the morning, at the Forty-Third Precinct. Shall we say, eight a.m.?"

I stared at Dehan for a moment. "That would be most helpful, Captain Jones. Thank you."

I hung up, and we sat staring at each other. Dehan spoke first. "What just happened, Stone?"

"Maybe that's what people are like in Maine. Maybe we've grown too accustomed to Babylon, Dehan."

She shook her head. "I thought I had a handle on this, but I'm losing it. I liked my theory about castration. It fit. A prostitution network came a close second, Stone. Now everything is broken, and I am not happy."

I thought about it for a while. "It still works. Both of them still work. I haven't read anywhere that Lieutenant Jones, now captain, was married or had kids. And if he found evidence of a prostitution ring, he may well have killed her and disposed of that evidence to preserve his family's honor."

"Family, huh?"

"Family. The statistics proved right again."

She sighed and rubbed her face, then looked at her watch.

"Come on, Stone. Let's go home. I'm going to make you a nice moussaka, to show how grateful I am you're not weird."

Mo snorted, but this time, for once, Dehan ignored him. We stood and put on our coats in silence and stepped out into the darkening evening, where it had started to rain.

SIX

Ewan Jones was a big man with not an ounce of fat on his body. He was six foot seven if he was an inch, and every inch was solid muscle. His hair, which had been sandy, was now a short, gray bristle, severely severed just above the ear. Below that line, his jaw was a slab of concrete which I was prepared to bet he shaved with a cut-throat razor and had never been close to anything as prissy as shaving soap, much less aftershave. I could hear him snarl in my mind, "What do men smell of?" And the reply from his devoted men, "Hard work and sweat, sir!"

His eyes were wide awake, curious, and penetrating, and that shade of pale blue that is almost white, evocative of ice, hard and cold. He stood as we walked into interview room three, gave Dehan a brief bow, and said, "Ma'am," then turned to me and said, "I am Captain Ewan Jones; are you Detectives Stone and Dehan?"

I smiled as we took our chairs, wondering whether the attempt to take immediate control of the situation was deliberate or automatic. I said, "Please, sit down, Captain." I showed him my badge, and Dehan flipped hers. "I am Detective John Stone; this is my partner, Detective Carmen Dehan. We are very grateful to you for coming to see us."

He sat and looked me square in the eye. His gaze was unsettling in its directness. "I was raised to understand the difference between right and wrong, Detective Stone. But sometimes the Lord tests us, by creating situations bewildering in their moral complexity, and it is hard to know where the true path of righteousness lies. When Sally was killed, I respected my family's wishes. We had disowned her, and when she was murdered, I took that as a sign that we had done the right thing. For she would have dragged us down with her."

He sighed and averted his eyes to stare at Dehan with that same direct, unwavering gaze. Then he went on, addressing her. "But not a day has gone by in the last nine years that I have not struggled with my conscience, wondering if I did in fact do the right thing, and I have come to believe that the Lord was not pleased with my decision. For, should not I have stayed with her to the last, offering her the chance of redemption? And if I had, might not I have saved her life? So when I heard on the news that you were reopening the case, I thought that perhaps the Lord was offering me a chance of redemption, where I failed to offer one to Sally."

Dehan gave an uncomfortable smile that involved only her mouth and nodded. "I am sure you have made the right decision this time, Captain Jones."

"The Good Lord will tell soon enough."

I decided to take back control before he had the three of us kneeling in prayer together.

"Captain, could you please talk us through the last time you saw Sally? And, was that the same occasion on which you went to see Gus?"

He nodded ponderously four times. "Yes, I can, and yes, it was." He picked up his polystyrene cup of coffee and examined the contents for a moment, then set it back down again.

"I come from a God-fearing family, Stone. We were among the first settlers in New England, Puritans and Pilgrims, and followers of the Word of God as spoken by Our Lord Jesus Christ.

As you must know yourselves . . ." He turned and nodded to Dehan, to include her in the pronoun. "We live in morally ambiguous times. In the name of tolerance, inclusion, and fairness, we allow every kind of moral deviation, every kind of outrage against Christian morality, and every kind of corruption and debasement of our children. Verily, evil walks among us, and too often it enjoys the protection of temporal law, when it flies in the face of Divine Law."

I smiled and nodded. "Captain, I appreciate that these are issues you feel very strongly about, but time is short, and we need to get to the facts of the case."

He held my eye for a beat, then said, "I'm getting there, Stone." He paused, as though gathering his thoughts. "I need you to understand how important the issue of Sally's behavior was to us. Our mom died when Sally was only a little girl, so she had no mother's guidance. Dad and I were military men, we were often absent, and so we were not there to guide her either. My brothers did what they could, but, looking back, I can see that she never had the love and support, and the guidance that a daughter needs if she is to avoid the paths of evil."

He spread out his strong hands on the table and studied them. I wondered how many people those hands had killed. He went on, looking at his hands now instead of us. "That's why, when my family decided to disown Sally, I was never really able to reconcile myself to the decision. Because, though my father and my brothers were adamant, I was not sure if . . ." He hesitated. "I mean to say that, I could see plain enough, like my father said, that her behavior was wicked and evil. But I was not sure if that behavior came from confusion through lack of guidance, or an evil rot in the heart. And if it was just confused behavior, then, surely, I should try to guide her back to righteousness."

Dehan said, "And that is why you started to visit her."

"That's correct." He nodded for a long while, until I was about to prompt him. Then, he spoke suddenly. "I came to see her three times. I pleaded with her. I begged her to get on her knees and pray with me, to beg for the Lord's forgiveness, for Him to shine some light on her path and guide her back into His fold." He shook his head and finally looked up and held my eye. "She laughed at me. Ever is the woman trapped in original sin. She quoted science at me, she mocked me and quoted studies and experiments, the alchemy of the Devil, to try to bring down my faith."

He turned to Dehan and regarded her like prosecuting counsel about to deliver the devastating conclusion to his closing argument. "Did you know, Detective Dehan, that Sir Isaac Newton, though raised an Anglican, revered Judaism and the Kabbalah, and that much of his understanding of gravity and mathematics was nothing more than a sinful application of his knowledge of alchemy, and the dark arts?"

She shook her head. "I didn't know that, but I think we are straying off task. Your sister refused to pray with you on three separate occasions. The last, I am guessing, would have been sometime in October 2010."

"You are correct," he said. "I arrived on October the eleventh, a Tuesday, because she had Tuesday off. We spent the day talking; that night, I tried to persuade her to pray with me. She became agitated and finally confessed that her boyfriend troubled her mind, and when she attempted to return to the straight and righteous path, he tempted her away. She asked me to leave her, to give her time, and she would return to the Lord. It was the most honest and sincere that I have ever seen her. She asked me also to go and see him. To beg him to leave her in peace to return to her faith."

Dehan was watching him with narrowed eyes. "She asked you to do that for her?"

"She did, and you can see why I have been in such turmoil these nine years."

I asked him, "And did you? Did you go and see him?"

"Yes, sir, I did. He had a garage, some kind of workshop where he customized bikes. His apartment was above the workshop, but when I went to see him that afternoon, on my way back home, I found him in his place of work. And I have to tell you, it was a crying shame and almost broke my heart. Here was a good man, who worked hard, and the quality of his work was some of the best I had ever seen. He was a real craftsman. Everything he had there, bikes and everything, was a real work of art, love, and attention to detail. Yet his soul was lost, and practically every panel and every gas tank I saw had some kind of diabolical emblem upon it."

"What happened?"

"I told him plain who I was and why I was there. He was courteous and told me he understood my position. He had the decency to say that in my position, he would do the same. He then, however, told me, very politely, to go to hell. I have to say I kind of liked the man, and told him that regretfully, that was where I would see him if he did not desist from pursuing my sister, Sally. Whereupon I left. The next thing I heard, Sally had been murdered." He shook his big head down at the table. "I'm pretty sure it wasn't him."

We both watched him a moment while he watched the tabletop. Then Dehan said, "But was it you?"

He blinked once, then remained perfectly immobile for five of the longest seconds I have ever lived through. Then he gave his head a small shake, blinked again, and frowned at Dehan. "Good Lord in heaven, it never occurred to me . . . You think I killed Sally . . ."

"We don't think anything, Captain Jones, but we are exploring all the possibilities. You have some pretty strict moral values . . ."

"And that is exactly what they are, Detective Dehan, and I hoped I had made that clear. They are Christian, moral values. I am neither judge nor executioner."

I cleared my throat. "Captain, perhaps you could explain to us a little about the Sacred Brotherhood of Christ. There was one time in their past, when they were founded, that they were both judges and executioners."

He grunted and made loose fists with which he gently pounded the table twice. "There was also a time, Stone, when the police would tie a man to a bentwood chair and beat him until he confessed to a crime he might or might not have committed. There was a time when the army used to whip and hang its men on little more than the whim of an officer. But the times have changed, and with them the institutions, great and small, of our nation."

"That is very true, but it doesn't answer my question. It just avoids it. When you referred earlier to your brothers, I know you have no biological brothers, so I assume that you were referring to your brothers in the Brotherhood."

"Indeed."

"And it was they, and your father, who decided to disown Sally. That must have been tantamount to an excommunication."

He nodded. "That would be a very close parallel, except it is worse. Because it requires the friends and the entire family to abide by the decree, and the person is disowned completely and entirely."

I scratched my chin. "Who takes the decision to disown somebody?"

"The Elder Brother in Council. In this case, it was Jeremiah Rose."

"And you and your father were required to abide by that decision and cut off all ties with Sally?"

"That's correct."

I drummed my fingers on the table. Captain Jones was looking distinctly uncomfortable. I said, "Captain, how powerful is the Brotherhood in Belfast?"

"I don't understand your question."

"How much weight do they pull? How many members are

there? How high are those members in the City Hall? Come on, Captain! You know exactly what I mean."

He sighed. "The Brotherhood has grown steadily in numbers, power, and influence over the last three hundred and fifty years. We are pretty powerful."

"So if the Brotherhood says jump and you don't jump, they can put hot coals under your feet, if you'll forgive the metaphor."

"Yeah, they can make you jump."

I shook my head and waved a hand. Dehan was watching me curiously. "Changing the subject briefly, on a separate matter. Back in the seventeenth and eighteenth centuries, if the Elder Brother in Council decreed that a certain person was touched by the Devil and was beyond redemption, what happened? How did that work?"

He sighed. "You've been doing your homework. I'll answer your question, though I have no doubt you have the answer already.

"When the witch hunts were at their peak in New England, in the late 1600s, the British authorities tried to assert control over what they saw as an outbreak of anarchy. If anybody was to be tried and executed, it should be done by the Crown, not by the people, because the Crown had the exclusive prerogative to use violence.

"So the Brotherhood, who derive their power directly from God via Jesus Christ Himself, devised a process in Council by which, once a person was identified as a servant of the Devil, an individual would be given the mission of executing the Council's sentence."

Dehan flopped back in her chair. "You mean they would tell one of their members to go and kill him or her."

"That is what it boils down to. Our governments do it every day, without the sanction of the Lord."

I sat forward. "So let me see if I have understood this correctly, Captain Jones. You had not had any contact with your sister for several years. During that time, her behavior, according to your standards and the standards of the Brotherhood, had grown progressively worse until you and the Brotherhood deemed she had become the whore of Babylon."

He nodded. "That's correct."

"So the Council was convened under Jeremiah Rose, and Sally was deemed irredeemably lost and sentenced to be disowned. And shortly after that, you went to see her three times, and after the third visit, she wound up dead."

"That about sums it up, Stone."

"So, I am going to put it to you that the Council and Jeremiah Rose in fact sentenced her to death, and you, being something of an expert in the field, were detailed by Mr. Rose to execute that sentence."

He stared at the wall opposite with no expression upon his face. "That is patently absurd."

Dehan frowned and shook her head. "I don't see what makes it absurd, and I don't see what makes it patently absurd. To me, it sounds like a very credible proposition." She put her elbows on the table and leaned forward. "Can you explain to us, Captain Jones, in what way exactly Detective Stone's proposition is absurd?"

"The Council no longer convenes for Hearings of Sentence of Death, nor Decrees of Execution. It hasn't done so for a hundred years."

I said, "The last was actually less than a hundred years ago, in 1921. Can you tell me, Captain Jones, when the Council decided finally to abolish Hearings of Sentence of Death and Decrees of Execution?"

He looked down at the tabletop. "No," he said simply.

"You can't?"

"No, I can't."

"Why is that, Captain?"

He closed his eyes and took a very deep breath. "Because, Detective Stone, they never were abolished. It was deemed wise, as we are the warriors of Christ, to keep that option open, though dormant, in case the need should ever arise to order an execution."

I watched him until he raised his eyes to meet mine. Then I asked him, "Was this one such case?"

He took his time answering, and I watched his muscles bunch and relax in his jaw. Finally, he said, "The Council thought it was."

SEVEN

"I was fifteen when she was born. That was something Pop never understood."

He fell silent so long, Dehan eventually said, "What was?"

He looked at her, almost surprised at her question. "That she was my little baby..."

Dehan flopped back in her chair. I felt my eyebrows rise up on my forehead, and after a second I stood, almost involuntarily. I walked to the wall and turned back to face him. "I think you need to explain that, Captain. You accepted a commission to kill the child you considered your own 'little baby'?"

He shook his head, two slow shakes. "I didn't say that."

I frowned.

Dehan said, "Well, what are you saying, Captain? Because I have to tell you, it is not at all clear. You had better start doing some explaining, Captain. Exactly what did the Council decide regarding Sally, and exactly what did they instruct you to do? And what exactly was the relationship between you and your sister?"

Again, he was quiet for a long time before answering. "She was my sister."

I said, quietly, "But she was more than that."

His voice seemed to shrink in his chest. "When Mom died, I

was nineteen. I was already a man, but it hit me hard. It hit us all hard. But it hit Sally the hardest. She was but four. Dad was away a lot. So was I, but not as much. Sally clung to me. She was the cutest little thing you ever did see. Sweet natured, loving, innocent ... She was my little baby."

His voice cracked, and he bit back the sobs, swallowing hard, clamping his jaw down on his own grief. We gave him a while, and he started talking again.

"Ours is a strict community, sworn to fight evil in the name of Jesus Christ. That's why I am a marine, and my father was before me. The Jones men have been military men for almost four hundred years, fighting evil in the Lord's name. When Sally started to go astray, I begged the Council to give her a chance. They didn't give her one, they gave her three, and every time, she reverted to her evil ways."

He looked me square in the eye with tears slipping down his cheeks.

"But she was still my little baby. May the Good Lord forgive me, I would do anything to save my baby girl. I have lived for two things in this life, Detective Stone, fighting the good fight for our Lord, and my little sister. Nothing else ever mattered to me. My faith in Jesus, and my love for my sister, have seen me through hell time and again. They were my twin lights in the darkness."

He sighed softly and looked down at his hands, cupped palm up on the table before him.

"When the Council finally ruled on Sally, they said that she had irredeemably set her face against the Lord and must be disowned. I felt my heart break and my faith was shaken."

"So what did you do?"

"That was when I came to see her the first time."

I returned to the table and leaned with my hands on the back of the chair. "Captain Jones, did the Council at any time instruct you, or request you, to kill your sister, Sally Jones?"

His pale eyes, despite the look of ice about them, were like two hot coals when he raised them to mine.

"I told you, the Council don't do that anymore."

"You also told me that, even though they were not de facto carried out, Hearings of Sentence of Death and Decrees of Execution were never abolished by the Council because it was deemed wise, as you were warriors of Christ, to keep that option open, in case the need should ever arise to order an execution. And you also told me that the Council considered Sally just such a case."

"That's true."

Dehan snapped, "So, am I going crazy here or are you contradicting yourself?"

He buried his face in his hands. "I argued that it would be murder, a very serious breach of the law, that the repercussions for the Brotherhood could be devastating. At first, they ignored me. They told me that because I was her brother, I should prove the strength of my faith by carrying out the sentence myself. But in the end, I managed to prevail upon them by stressing the fact that, whoever carried out the deed, everyone and anyone involved in the conspiracy would be equally guilty. That gave them pause. They dismissed me . . ."

"When was this?"

He raised his face from his hands, thought a moment, and shook his head. "I don't recall the exact date, but it was the first few days of October."

I asked, "What happened then?"

"I was told by a friend—I won't tell you their name—that the Council dispatched two Brothers to talk to Sally. The idea was they would tell her exactly how things stood, and warn her that she was treading a fine line, and the Council would not tolerate any further excesses."

I pulled out the chair and sat again. "But you don't know for sure whether they did that or not . . ."

He dismissed that with a shake of his head. "I am certain they did. It's exactly the sort of thing they would do. I have no confirmation, I can't prove it, but I know they did it."

Dehan was staring hard at him through screwed-up eyes, like

she was trying to force him into focus. "Are you telling us that you think the Council went ahead with Sally's execution despite your warnings?"

"I don't know. At first I thought so, and I went and had it out with Jeremiah. He said they had only warned her. And . . ."

"And what?"

"There should have been fire. The hands and the feet, the multiple stabbings . . . That is not how they do it . . ." He glanced at me. "Not how they would do it."

I said, "How would they do it?"

"There would be fire, to purify the soul."

She looked away at the wall, then back at him, and snapped, "I'm going to need the names of those Brothers!"

"I don't know their names."

Her hand came down hard on the table, and she pointed her finger at him like a revolver. "Then I want the names of each and every damned member of the Sacred Brotherhood of Christ! And I want them now!"

He nodded, and suddenly he looked broken and small. "I can do that. Yes, I can do that."

She got up and left the room, slamming the door behind her. He didn't seem to notice. He studied each wall in turn, like a man who has only just realized he is living in a prison.

"It was never intended to be evil. The intention was to do good, in the name of Jesus . . ."

"I am no philosopher, Captain Jones, but it seems common sense to me that good is just a name we each give to something different, and so is evil. If good is unquestioning obedience to a god, and that god, or more likely one of his priests, orders you to rape and torture all the women in some village in the Congo, then good is clearly a cruel, heartless thing that has nothing to do with compassion or kindness. And if evil is disobedience to that god, then any person who, through compassion and empathy, tries to help those women, is evil, and our understanding of good and evil is stood upon its head. Good in that case is just another word for obedience, and evil is simply disobedience."

He frowned at me, not in anger, but as though struggling to understand. "You think there is more to good and evil than obedience to God?"

I shrugged. "I think the words are meaningless, Captain Jones, unless you put them in a context." I spread my hands. "A good Christian, a good fisherman, a good chef, a good driver . . ."

"But a person's moral condition . . . ?"

"Like I said, I am not a philosopher. I get by with being kind wherever I can. If there is a great judgment to be faced, then I'll cross that bridge when I get to it. The question we are facing here and now is not about God, it's about Sally, and somebody who stole her life. And I think you know who that somebody was."

He was expressionless for a long while, staring at me. Then the door opened and Dehan came in with a pad of ruled, A4 paper and a pen. She dropped them on the table in front of Jones and said, "Write, Captain. A full statement, and all the names of the damned Council!"

He said nothing but took the paper and the pen and began to write.

I stepped outside and strolled down to the coffee machine, dialing the Montefiore Hospital in Westchester. When I got through, I told them who I was and said, "I need to know if a Sally Jones was seen by or admitted to your ER department in the first two weeks of October 2010."

She told me she'd put me through to the records department, and when Records answered, it was a woman who sounded like everybody's mother.

"You understand I can only give you very limited information . . ."

"I know that, ma'am. All I need to know is if she was admitted and if her injuries, such as they were, were consistent with having been beaten."

"I can't offer an opinion on that, Detective Stone, I am not an ME..."

"Let me give you her Social Security number. Please retrieve any files you have on her and give me what details you can of her injuries. I'm not going to call you as a witness. If this goes any further, it will be the ME I call on, not you, honey."

I read her the number and heard the keys rattle. When she spoke again, she had a smile in her voice. "Do you know how inappropriate it is to call a woman 'honey' in the workplace?"

"No, do you?"

She repressed a squeal of laughter, then went serious. "Okay, I have her here... First two weeks of October two thousand...?"

"And ten."

She was quiet then for a good while. Then she said, "How can I put this to you? She was admitted twice in that two-week period, on the fifth and the seventh. On both occasions, she complained that she had tripped and fallen in the bath. And to the nature of her bruising, and the recommendations the doctors made on examining those bruises, that I think you should... should get a court order to view them."

"You have been extremely helpful."

"Well, it has been my pleasure... honey."

We both laughed, and I hung up.

I returned to the interrogation room just as Jones was handing over his statement to Dehan. I leaned on the table and stared deeply into those pale blue eyes.

"Who beat her up, Jones? You, or your brothers?"

His eyes shifted away to look at the wall. "They did."

"How many times?"

"Twice. The Tuesday and the Thursday. How did you know?"

"Because she was so badly hurt, she wound up in the ER!"

He closed his eyes and pinched the bridge of his nose. "It was a last-ditch attempt at exorcizing the evil that was within her. But it was too late."

Dehan snarled, "What do you mean, it was too late?"

"She had already recruited the Devil's henchman. That was what they said."

"Who the hell was the Devil's henchman? Jesus! How crazy are you people?"

"They said she had recruited a Hells Angel. I always assumed it was Gus; even though he was not a Hells Angel, they would not have made that fine distinction. They would have seen him simply as one of the Devil's henchmen."

I sighed, bit back my anger, and said, "You can go, Captain Jones, but make yourself available for further questioning."

He nodded and stood.

I held up my hand, still looking down at the tabletop. "When the time comes, Captain Jones, will you be prepared to testify against the Brotherhood in court?"

He stared at me for a long time, then lowered his gaze to the floor. "Yes," he said. "I will."

Then he turned and left, leaving the interrogation room door open behind him.

Dehan shifted in her chair to look up at me. "Stone, have you any idea what the hell is going on?"

I didn't answer straightaway. I wasn't sure what answer to give her. Eventually, I said, "This is conspiracy to murder across state lines. We need to hand it over to the Feds." I felt a hot coal in my belly and scowled. "We have no idea how many other people these bastards have beaten, tortured, and even killed."

She watched me a moment and gave a soft grunt. "We need to talk to the chief, Stone. Maybe we can cooperate with Belfast PD and make some headway on our own before we need to call in the Feds. We don't know yet how far their activities spread outside Belfast. It may be they were limited to Maine and New York. If that's the case, we don't need to call them in at all."

I considered her a moment where she sat on the hard chair, frowning up at me. I was struck for the thousandth time by her extraordinary beauty, internal and external. I smiled. "Okay, let's go talk to him."

I stood, but she remained sitting. "Are we sure?"

I frowned. "About what?"

"I don't know, Stone. A religious cult conspiring to murder people who stray from the path of the Lord . . ."

"Most motives for murder are pretty crazy when you say them like that, Dehan." I gave a small laugh. "Killed his wife because she slept with a young man . . . ? Killed a shopkeeper for ten bucks and a bottle of whiskey . . . ?"

"Okay, wiseass, let's go talk to the chief. But you'll see what I mean when we talk this through. It is not cut and dried."

I nodded. "I know. I'm not one hundred percent comfortable either. But what we have is pretty compelling."

She shook her head. "No, Stone. You know I am usually one hundred percent with you in your assessments . . ."

"No, you're not. You always have a theory of your own."

She shrugged and nodded. "Yeah, that's true. But in this case, I have to tell you, you are way off base. The evidence we have is compelling, to the point of being probative, that there is a crazy cult in Belfast that at one time went around killing witches and warlocks. It is not compelling at all as far as Sally is concerned."

I made a face and shrugged. "Let's go talk to the inspector."

EIGHT

We climbed the stairs and knocked on the inspector's door.

"Come!"

We pushed in, and he turned from the bonsai on his windowsill, where he was watering it. He made a brave attempt to stop the smile fading from his face when he saw that it was us.

"John! Carmen!" He said it like he was greeting us at a cocktail party. "Always so nice. Sit, please. I imagine you have news on the Sally Jones case."

We sat, and I placed Captain Jones' statement in front of him.

"Essentially, sir, he admits to being a member of the Sacred Brotherhood of Christ, a three-hundred-year-old Christian cult who were dedicated to exorcizing, punishing, and killing those who strayed from the straight and narrow path of Jesus, according to their interpretation of that path. He claims that the Council, headed by one Jeremiah Rose, ruled to have Sally Jones 'disowned.' Exactly what that means, and how far it goes, is ambiguous. But he did state that the Brotherhood never abolished their self-granted right to sentence a member to death, and execute that member, so that they would always have that option open for exactly such a case as Sally's."

The inspector gazed over at his bonsai with a certain amount of longing. "A seventeenth-century sect of Christian assassins . . . ?"

"That's about the size of it, sir."

"Conspiring and killing across state borders?"

I hesitated. "Yes, sir."

A faint smile touched his face. "In that case, we can hand it over to the bureau, let them deal with the mess, and still take credit for solving the case."

Dehan cleared her throat. "Actually, sir, I don't think it's that cut and dried. If I may, I think there are some points that we need to bear in mind."

He tore his eyes away from the bonsai and frowned at her. "Indeed? Such as . . . ?"

"To begin with, Captain Jones never expressly stated that the Brotherhood had issued an order of execution, or even a sentence of death, against Sally. In fact, at one point, he seemed to say they had not. It is true that members of the Brotherhood visited her on two occasions, on October fifth and seventh, and on both of those occasions she wound up in the ER, but from what I understand, her injuries were not life-threatening . . . ?" She made the statement a question and asked me with her face.

I nodded. "They were not, but we need a court order to see the medical reports."

He made a note, and Dehan went on. "If there was an order of execution, however crazy they are, they are not going to beat her up and walk away twice, leaving her free to go to the hospital or the cops, and then come 'round a third time and kill her! I mean, they may be crazy enough to belong to the sect, but let's remember that we are talking about the local doctor, the bank manager, the local attorney, the guy who runs the auto dealership. Maybe even the sheriff or some of his deputies. They may be living out a fantasy, but they are sane enough to hold down jobs and run businesses."

The inspector glanced at me. "That is your kind of reasoning, John, and I have to say it makes sense."

I nodded, but before I could say anything, Dehan was talking again.

"And there is another point, sir. We don't know how many members there are in the sect, but the Council members he has listed here are twelve, and we know that the sect has been growing steadily over the years. Conspiracies are typically between two or three people. Anything over five becomes highly risky. But here"—she pointed at the captain's statement—"we have a conspiracy to murder involving a minimum of twelve people. That seems to me to be entering the realm of the absurd."

The inspector nodded slowly several times. Finally, he said, "So we have to bring the Council members in."

She was answering before he had finished. "We do, sir! But we have to do so resigned to the fact that we will not find Sally's killer there. We will find the people who beat her, but not the ones who murdered her."

I frowned. "You seem pretty convinced of that, Dehan."

"I am, totally. I will put my hand in the fire and state that the Brotherhood did not kill Sally Jones." She turned back to the inspector. "So, sir, I would ask that for the present we cooperate with Belfast PD. How?" She asked her own question and answered it. "We send them a copy of the captain's statement, outlining the background to the case, and ask them to pull in the Council members, question them, and get statements from them, and from there proceed on an information-sharing basis until it becomes clear that there is a real case to pursue, here or there, and then consider the possibility of joint interrogations and arrests here and there, if it's necessary."

The inspector turned to me. "John?"

I nodded. "Yes, sir. It makes sense to me." I turned to Dehan. "But I have to say that I am curious. Do you have a prime suspect of your own? What's your thinking?"

She shifted in her chair and looked a little uncomfortable.

"Frankly, I don't think we have enough solid evidence yet, but what is clear to me is that Sally Jones was a girl who went around stirring up a lot of strong feelings in people, and most of those feelings were within the sexual-territorial spectrum. And, I am still not convinced that she wasn't involved in some kind of illegal or illicit activity. I don't know what, but I can smell it."

The inspector grunted. "We don't solve homicides with the sense of smell, Detective Dehan."

"No, sir, I know. But I am pretty sure that the activities of Captain Jones and the Brotherhood are symptomatic of the kind of chaos she used to go around stirring up, rather than causal of her death."

He smiled at me and raised an eyebrow. "Very nicely put. John . . . ?"

I smiled at Dehan. "I am happy to hold off on informing the Feds until we have something more concrete, and I am happy to collaborate and share with Belfast PD. Meanwhile, we can also explore other angles."

"Such as?"

Dehan answered before I had a chance. "There are two things that I would like to do, sir, Stone." She glanced at us each in turn. "There are a couple of boxes of her things down in evidence. The case was never closed, and there was nobody to return them to, so they are still sitting there. I'd like to go through them. There may be a clue there as to what she was doing and who else was involved in her life."

The inspector nodded. "Makes sense. And . . . ?"

"I think it is high time we went and had a talk with Gus."

I nodded. "I agree. He keeps popping up, and Captain Jones admits going to see him very shortly before Sally died."

He spread his hands. "Very good. Carry on, then. Carmen seems to have her finger on the pulse in this one, John. I hope you'll listen to her."

"Of course. I always do, sir."

"Splendid, well, keep me posted and let's hope you can bring it to a speedy conclusion, as usual."

He smiled warmly at us as we left, and I fell in beside Dehan on the stairs.

"Box of stuff down in evidence. Good call."

She smiled briefly. "Thanks. I hope you didn't mind . . ."

"Not at all! It's about the case. And Gus, high time . . ."

"No bruised male ego, anything like that . . . ?"

I gave a small laugh and shook my head. "No, no, not at all. My mother and her wife beat all that out of me back in the early seventies, when I was still struggling with the Oedipal phase. I had no father to kill but two mothers . . . It got very complicated. They were about to throw me on a bonfire along with their bras, but I was rescued by a band of Buddhist chipmunks who explained to me that I had not really lost my ego, I'd never really had one to start with. Then *Star Wars* was released and I realized that Yoda was my true master."

By now, we were standing by the elevators, waiting to go down to the evidence basement. She was staring at me without expression.

"Buddhist chipmunks . . ."

I nodded. "Uh-huh."

The elevator arrived, pinged, and the doors slid open. It was empty, and we stepped in. As the doors closed, she said, "That is bullshit, Stone. You have to stop this childish fantasizing. Everybody knows that chipmunks are Taoists. If you're going to lie, at least do your homework."

"You're a very hard woman, Detective Dehan. Very hard."

We stepped out into a small, tiled stairwell with a couple of fire doors on the right. We pushed through them and found ourselves in a small room with counters running across the back wall, enclosed in bulletproof glass. There were small, arched holes in the glass, so you could talk to people's belly buttons on the other side. A small guy with big eyes on the other side leered at Dehan.

"Good morning, Detective Dehan, what can I do for you today?"

"Jones, Sally, thirteenth of October 2010. She has a couple of boxes of personal effects. I need to see them."

"You can't take them out."

"Gee, I didn't know that. Did you know that, Stone? Nobody ever told me that in the last fifteen years. I want to see them. I don't want to take them home and play with them. I want to see them. *Es, ee, ee*. See."

He seemed unperturbed and kept smiling at her with a mouth like a wet keyhole. "I'll let you in and lead you to the evidence boxes." He scowled at me. "What about you?"

"What about me?" Before he could answer, I asked, "What's your hometown again, Oswald?"

He unlocked the steel mesh door and stood back, frowning at me. "Antler, in North Dakota, why?"

We followed him down a long, narrow passage between gray steel shelves crammed with cartons, crates, and boxes. I spoke over Dehan's head to his retreating form.

"I just heard on the news. Two trucks carrying dehydrated water collided there and the town is flooded."

"Jeeez! Seriously?"

"Seriously. No casualties, but you better go check it out."

"I will, thanks."

He showed us her stuff and hurried away. We took the carton and the plastic crate and carried them to a blue table made of Formica and steel tubing and settled ourselves there to examine what there was.

What there was, was not a lot. A few items of clothing, less than you would expect, and though it was stuff that could look sexy on the right woman, it was not of itself revealing or of a provocative design: a couple of pairs of boot cut jeans, some sweatshirts, underwear that was more pretty than it was sexy, a couple of dresses, and not much more in the way of clothes.

There were toiletries, lots of them, and we went through those with care, though in the end we found nothing of interest among them either. Then there were the ornaments: everything from tiny pillboxes and silver candelabras to teddy bears and music boxes. There were CDs too, mostly of bands I had never heard of, and DVDs of romantic comedies and European films in which the silences were more important than the sparse snatches of dialogue. Her books were eclectic, Zen, Jeet Kune Do, *Bridget Jones's Diary*, several "think positive" self-help books. There was also a laptop, which Dehan fired up and started exploring.

A couple of grunts and a peculiar frown made me ask, "You found something?"

She shook her head. "No, no, nothing."

Eventually, she closed down the laptop, sighed, and pulled out a Tupperware box of opaque plastic with an orange lid. It was about a foot long, five inches across, and three or four inches deep. Through the dull, semitransparent sides I could see junk, but not much more. She opened it and took out a comb, a lipsalve, a couple of pens, some bits of paper, and then she stopped. Something about the way she did it made me stop and watch her. She was looking at a photograph, maybe five by three.

She stared at it so long, I said, "What is it?"

"I don't know."

"What do you mean, Dehan? Talk to me."

She didn't say anything, but after another five seconds, she handed me the photograph.

It was recognizable as Sally. She was in jeans and a sweatshirt, two items we had just looked at. She had her hair tied back in a loose ponytail, and she was sitting on the hood of a Mustang, squinting slightly, smiling at the camera.

In front of her, leaning his ass against the hood, was the stereotypic biker-cum-Hells-Angel. He was tall, maybe six-two, athletically built, muscular, with a full beard and moustache and long, fair hair. He was wearing jeans and cowboy boots, and a denim jacket with the sleeves torn off. There were no Angels emblems visible anywhere.

They were in the forecourt of a garage or a workshop, and in the background, I could see a couple of hogs.

I stared at the picture for a long time while Dehan stared at me. Finally, I handed it back and said, "Gus?"

"Two gets you twenty, as you might say."

I gave a small shrug and shook my head. "I can see you think this is important, Dehan, but I am not seeing it myself."

"The car."

"What about it?"

"The license plate."

"You can't see the license plate. It's behind his legs."

She sighed and looked at me with a face that said I was being deliberately obtuse. I raised my eyebrows and shook my head in a way that said I wasn't.

"No," she said. "You can't read the plate. I can!"

"You're reaching."

"Maybe, but in this case we need to reach, because if we don't, we might as well contemplate our navels and hope for enlightenment."

I made a noise that was part sigh and part grunt and ended up sounding like a groan. "Well, I wouldn't mind contemplating your navel until enlightenment struck, but mine doesn't appeal as much. What might be a better plan, which should satisfy both of us, is if we go to Gus' workshop on Westchester and White Plains and ask him about the photograph. It's about time we spoke to him anyway."

She took out her cell and made a copy of the photograph. Then she held up the phone and waved it at me. "I want to know where that car is, how he got hold of it, and who—or whom—he sold it to."

"You're reading too much into it. He deals in Harleys and muscle cars, Dehan. And he has a classic, iconic picture of his girl on the hood of his Mustang, just as she might have been on the back of his hog. It would be like you or I having a picture taken at Niagara Falls."

She tapped the photograph with her finger. "I want to know where this car is. Period."

NINE

It was no more than a ten-minute drive from the station house, east along Story and then north up White Plains, to Gus' Repair Shop. It stood on the corner of White Plains and Westchester. It was back from the road a bit, tucked in behind the gas station, so that if you weren't really looking for it, you might miss it altogether.

He had a big, asphalt lot out front, and we pulled in, cutting across the traffic, and parked in the lot. There were no other cars there, or bikes, and when we climbed out of the Jag into the blustery wind and the slight drizzle, we saw that the steel blind was down, and some kid had put a rock through the apostrophe in GUS' REPAIR SHOP. So now, without the Saxon genitive, it sounded like pidgin English.

We walked around back, where we found much the same, plus a couple of rusted gas tanks, and peered in through a small window. All we found was irrefutable evidence that Gus was no longer there, and hadn't been for some time.

We took a stroll over to the gas station and asked around, but the staff there was as transient as the clientele. Nobody remembered the shop ever being open.

On the far side of the lot, on the corner with the exit from the freeway, there was a three-story clapboard house with a burgundy awning that said it was a home care service. We made the walk, back across the wet asphalt, with Dehan fingering strands of cold, damp hair from her face, and came to the small offices of Angele's Caring. I pushed through the door, and Dehan closed out the damp behind me. There were two desks and the slightly stuffy warmth of electric radiators. Two women sat behind the desks. They were both in their early fifties. The one nearest the door was watching us. She was black and large and wore glasses that magnified her pupils to twice their size. I figured she was the receptionist-cum-secretary.

The other was of the same age, a little too well groomed, with black, permed hair and a moderately expensive suit. She glanced at us, then continued to read the papers in front of her.

The woman with the glasses said, "Good morning, how may I help you?"

I showed her my badge. "I'm Detective John Stone; this is my partner, Detective Dehan. We are making inquiries about Gus' Repair Shop next door."

By this time, the woman in the suit had raised her eyes from her papers and was watching us. The two women glanced at each other. Then the suit said, "Gus' workshop has been closed for about ten years." She frowned. "I'd have thought you'd know that."

Dehan frowned at her. "Is this business yours?"

"Yes. I'm Angeles Budia, I own this business. What is this about?"

"You were here ten years ago?"

"I've been here for twenty years. You mind telling me why you're asking these questions?"

I answered her. "Ms. Budia, we are a cold-case unit, and we are investigating a murder that was committed back in 2010. We think that Gus could have information that would help us in our investigation. If you know where he is, we would be very grateful if you would tell us how we can contact him."

She watched me say all that, then narrowed her eyes and stared over at her receptionist. Her receptionist shrugged, chuckled, and muttered, "Don't ask me!"

I could feel Dehan getting antsy. "What's the joke?"

Angeles flopped back in her chair and laced her fingers over her belly. She stared at Dehan with eyes that were not easily intimidated. "The joke?" she asked. "You want to know what the joke is? I'll tell you, Detective Dehan. The joke is the NYPD, and the punch line is the Forty-Third Precinct."

I saw Dehan's cheeks color and cut in. "You care to explain that, Ms. Budia? In particular, how it relates to Gus."

She shifted her eyes to meet mine, and I could see real anger in them. "Sure, I care to explain, Detective Dehan. Gus Angus McBride was one of the good guys. He liked to play the tough biker, he had tattoos of the death's head and all that crap, and he liked to look dangerous. But underneath—and not so far underneath—he was a good, kind, hard-working guy." She pointed around. "This neighborhood is full of *pendejos* selling drugs, weed, coke, heroin! And you guys ignore it to keep yourselves safe and half of you are takin' bribes and protection from the sellers. I know this!" She thumped her chest with her fist. "I seen this, with my own eyes. But one guy, one decent, hard-working guy, because you don't like the way he dresses, you don't like that he is a little bit of an anarchist . . ." She thrust her hands at me like she was trying to push me away. "Ah! You make me sick!"

Dehan's face had changed. It had softened. She leaned on the desk and held Angeles' eye. "Angeles, what happened?"

Angeles leaned forward, her face flushed and her eyes bright with anger. She half screamed in Dehan's face. "He was murdered! And it was never investigated!" She made the face of cops everywhere who don't give a damn. "'He was just another Angel wannabe, probably selling drugs, some lowlife, who cares? They done the city a favor!' *Hijos de puta!* Now you come around here, ten years later, and you don't even know he was murdered?"

Dehan turned and stared at me.

I gave a single nod. "We need to pull the case file."

Dehan looked back at Angeles. "Thank you for your time, Ms. Budia."

We stepped out of the office and into the gray drizzle, clutching what dignity we had left with our tails firmly between our legs. We drove back to the station house in a silence accentuated by the rhythmic squeak and thud of the windshield wipers.

Then, as we turned into Story Avenue, Dehan shook her head and said, "I don't buy it." Then she looked at me with a face that asked me to say I didn't buy it either.

I glanced at her and shrugged. "When does murder make sense?" I looked back at the road and spun the wheel into Fteley Avenue, where I pulled into the parking lot. "It's a crime because it doesn't make sense."

She snorted. "It's a crime because the state reserves to itself the right to violence."

I raised an eyebrow at her. "The state reserves to itself the right to senseless violence. Violence in self-defense, for example, is legal, smart-ass. My point is, you're looking for reason and coherence in an act that is inherently insane. I believe I am quoting you, by the way."

She sighed. "It wouldn't be the first time."

She opened the door and climbed out. I climbed out after her, and she leaned on the roof to look at me. Small droplets of water gathered on her hair. "Okay, sensei, I take your point, but even within the inherent madness of murder, you and I know that it is always driven by either sex or money."

"Not always."

"Okay, not always, but somewhere in the region of ninety-nine percent of the time. And the remainder are either serial killers or some form of aberration."

I gave a small shrug and decided not to ask her why this could not be an aberration. Instead, I asked, "Okay, what's your point?"

"My point . . ." She sighed and looked over at the entrance to the station house, chewing her lip. "What is the motive? That she has strayed from a religious path which stopped killing people a hundred years ago or more?" She pointed at me. "Tell me Captain Ewan Jones killed her and I'll buy it. I can buy that this guy is riddled with weird Freudian impulses about his sister. I can buy that he was consumed with feelings of betrayal and dark, incestuous guilt, that could lead him to punish her. And the removal of the hands and feet definitely plays into that. But a whole council? A bunch of twelve guys with no personal axe to grind? It just doesn't ring true, Stone."

I drummed my fingers on the burgundy roof of the car, watching the ripples move through the small pools gathered there. I nodded a few times, then sighed myself. "Yes. I agree. But as I have said from the beginning. We have to let the evidence dictate. Until now, according to your idea, we have followed the theories to find the evidence." I pointed back at her. "And it worked. But I think we have reached a point where we have to start letting the evidence lead the way." I shook my head and wiped accumulated droplets from my eyes and face with my fingers. "We don't know anything about this council. We don't know anything about how close they were with the Jones family. Your objections are founded on suppositions, Dehan. Right now, we need to pull the file on the Angus McBride murder and see what it says, and then we need to go and talk to Jeremiah Rose and his Brothers, because what it looks like right now is that he and his boys, with the possible help of Ewan Jones, killed both Sally and Gus."

She bumped her fist softly, twice, on the roof of the Jag. "Yup. That is what it looks like. Okay, big guy, let's go."

We crossed the wet blacktop to the station, and while Dehan went to find some coffee, I ran Angus McBride through the system. He showed up as a cold case, and I pulled the two boxes of files from under the desk and started rifling through them. It turned out to be the bottom one of four lying flat under all the ones that were stacked upright.

By that time, Dehan had returned, put a cup of coffee in front of me, and said, "Huh, a cold case. Not a surprise, I guess."

She dropped into her chair and crossed her ankles on the corner of the desk. I opened the file and looked at the photographs of a big, athletic guy in jeans. He had bare arms and a denim jacket with the sleeves torn off. His hair was fair and long and he had a goatee. On his left shoulder, he had a Baphomet tattooed.

He was lying on his back. Close-ups showed a small hole above his heart. His eyes were open, his expression surprised, his mouth slightly open.

I tossed them over to Dehan and started reading.

"Angus McBride, thirty-two, yadda yadda address, blah blah. Found by Angel Rodriguez on the morning of the thirteenth of October 2010 . . ." I raised my eyes and stared at Dehan.

She puffed out her cheeks and looked away.

I went on reading. ". . . in the entrance hall of his apartment above his workshop on White Plains Avenue. Cause of death as per ME's report, a single gunshot wound to the heart with a nine-millimeter pistol. Weapon was not recovered. There were no signs that the lock had been picked or entry had been otherwise forced. His position in the hall, opposite the front door, suggests he had opened the door just prior to being shot. There was no significant forensic evidence in the form of fingerprints, DNA, or ballistics. CCTV cameras in the lot proved to be inoperative. Interviews with neighbors revealed that nobody saw or heard anything during that night.

"Time of death estimated at between ten thirty Thursday night, when he was last seen at the Waddling Duck on Westchester Avenue, and nine thirty on Thursday morning, when he was found by Mr. Rodriguez."

"Eleven hours. Let me get this clear in my head . . ." She rubbed her face with her hands and stared at the ceiling. "Sally was working that night."

"Yeah, she closed the bar early at roughly one a.m. and headed home."

"So the time frame for her murder is a little tighter than Gus', but pretty much the same."

I nodded. "Yeah."

"And we know that both directly and indirectly, both victims were threatened by the Sacred Brotherhood of Christ . . ."

"She for being the whore of Babylon, and he for being the henchman of the Devil."

She screwed up her eyes like she had mental constipation and put her fingertips to her forehead. "Stone, wait. Are we really, really saying that twelve grown men in Belfast, Maine, sentenced a man and a woman to death because they were living in a way they did not approve of, not just in another city, but a different state! Are we really saying that?"

"No, we are saying the circumstantial evidence suggests that there is an intimate connection between the two murders, and they may have been committed by the same person. Circumstantial evidence also suggests that the Sacred Brotherhood of Christ might have had some involvement."

She groaned. "Okay, okay, you're right."

"I won't say the evidence, Dehan, because this is not a rule. But I will say that the evidence is there for a reason. The chances they both died on the same night by coincidence are so remote as to be insignificant. The chances they died within a few hours of each other by coincidence are equally remote. By the same token, the chances that their murders are connected are conversely high." I spread my hands. "The Council have to go to the top of our list of suspects, A, because we know that they had a vested interest—however absurd—in stopping Sally in her evil ways, and B . . ." I smiled. "Because we have no other suspects, aside from Ewan, and he is intimately tied in with the Council. We can't just say, 'The evidence points to an absurd motive, therefore we shall ignore it.' The motive may seem absurd to us, but what is important or rational is totally subjective, Dehan. You know that. Besides, what you describe as an absurd motive has triggered innumerable wars and caused the deaths of hundreds of millions of people over the years."

Her sigh was noisy and through the nose. "Fine, point taken. So how the hell do we proceed from here?"

I dropped the file on the desk and drummed the arm of my chair with my fingertips. "We wait for a reply from Belfast PD, and we interview the Council—at the very least we interview Jeremiah Rose—and see where that interview leads us. We could really use some physical evidence."

Dehan kind of winced. "We have another problem as far as physical evidence is concerned."

I knew what she was going to say and nodded.

"The MOs, Stone. Two murders committed on the same night, within a few hours of each other, and within half a mile of each other; two people who were romantically and sexually involved with each other, and yet the MOs are not just different, they are radically different."

"I know. She was brutalized, quite literally destroyed, and he was executed with a single shot to the heart. Probably by somebody he knew."

I picked up a piece of paper, screwed it into a little ball, and threw it at her. She caught it left-handed, and I picked up a pencil and wagged it at her.

"You, Ritoo Glasshopper, who are so fond of theorizing, put this in your pipe and ponder the metaphorical smoke."

"Wow, how could I resist? Hit me, Sensei."

"Gus was, and I quote, a henchman of the devil. The Brotherhood hit man, be it Ewan or one of the others, it makes no difference, drops by to see him, ostensibly for a chat, but in reality so that Ewan will know him next time he sees him. They talk, and our killer departs, apparently mollified, reassured, whatever."

She was frowning, curious. "Okay . . ."

"A couple of nights later, he comes back and rings on the bell. Gus looks through the spy hole, recognizes him, and opens the door. Our guy pops him through the heart, closes the door, and leaves. This is, after all, a mere execution of the henchman who is helping, or protecting, Sally, according to the Brotherhood."

"Huh..."

"Now he goes—and for my money, we are talking about her brother—to her apartment. He knows she is sleeping, and he also knows that at this time of night, she will not let him in, either because she's had a bellyful of him or because she suspects what's coming. So he picks the lock, creeps into her room, and now unleashes not just his religious fervor, but his own personal passions too. And that, my dear Watson, is the reason for the two different MOs."

TEN

It was a six-and-a-half-hour drive from the Bronx to Belfast. We got the okay from the chief at eleven a.m. Belfast PD were happy to cooperate with us in any way they could. In fact, they were so keen that the chief, Patrick McFarlane, had asked that I liaise directly with him.

We'd set out at twelve noon, aiming to arrive about six thirty that evening, and Dehan had called when we were on the I-95 and past New Rochelle. The drizzle had turned to cold Atlantic rain, and the wipers were working overtime. She put her phone on speaker.

"McFarlane!"

"Good afternoon, Chief McFarlane. This is Detective John Stone from the Forty-Third in the Bronx. I'm here with my partner, Detective Dehan. We're on our way, just leaving New York, and should be with you by six thirty p.m."

"Uh-huh, just come straight to the station house, I'll still be here. We'll talk then."

"I have a couple of questions, Chief, if you have a moment."

"Make 'em quick."

"You brought in any of the Brothers yet?"

"Nope. I want to talk to you guys before I do that. What else?"

"How big of a cheese is Jeremiah Rose in Belfast—or in Maine for that matter?"

"You guys drink beer?"

"We've been known to."

"Okay, we'll go to Darby's. They have some good beers there. See you six thirty, sharp."

He hung up, and Dehan sat staring at the phone, pursing her lips. "I know," she said, "that you think I am too eager to jump to conclusions..."

"I have never said that."

"But you have implied it on more than one occasion, and I am inclined to agree."

"However..."

"However, on this occasion, I believe he just told us that Jeremiah Rose is a big, bad old Stilton."

"I think so, Dehan."

After that, we talked mainly, and sporadically, about the landscape, about the naked skeletons of the deciduous trees against the gunmetal clouds, and the fat, bulbous evergreens in the forests. At one thirty, we stopped for a roadside lunch of burgers and coffee, and then pressed on through the wet afternoon into the dark evening, where everything through the windshield was either shiny black or a distorted, liquid glow, and the pine woods on either side of the road loomed like the vast walls of immense tunnels.

At six thirty-five, we pulled up outside the old, two-story redbrick building that was the Belfast PD station house. We climbed out of the car and hunched into our shoulders as we crossed the sidewalk and pushed through the glass door. The desk sergeant, who had red hair and freckles and looked like somebody's girlfriend, smiled at us.

"You must be the detectives from New York."

I agreed we must, and she picked up the internal phone. "Chief, your New York visitors are here. Shall I . . ." She looked up at us with very blue eyes while she listened, then said, "Okay," and hung up. "He'll be right down. Please, take a seat. Though I guess maybe you have sore asses from so much sitting all the way from New York."

She wrinkled her nose and giggled, so I wrinkled my nose too and giggled back. By the time I had arched an eyebrow in response to Dehan's withering look, Chief Pat McFarlane came tripping down the stairs, pulling on a brown coat and ramming an old, blue trilby hat on his head. He came through the door into the lobby, said, "Stone, Dehan. We'll go in my car." He pushed past us out into the rain. We followed, but he kept talking, without looking at us. "Wait here. I'll bring the car 'round."

And with that, he was gone, running toward the parking lot with his collar turned up.

Dehan gave me a small frown. "Didn't the Addams Family live in Maine?"

I smiled. "If they don't, they should."

He emerged from the gloom of the parking lot a couple of minutes later in a cream Honda, which was easily forty years younger than my car but looked easily forty years older. We climbed in and crawled two hundred yards to Darby's tavern on High Street. Stopped at the lights at the intersection, he uttered the only words he spoke on the short, slow journey.

"I like to lead by example."

I nodded like I understood and wondered if that qualified as a lie. I decided it probably did.

He pulled up outside a double-fronted redbrick with a green, wooden façade on the ground floor, and we climbed out and loped into the firelit warmth of the restaurant. There was nobody else there, so we grabbed a table by the fire and ordered three burgers and three pints of cloudy, brown beer that looked and tasted like it was intended to be enjoyed by Thor.

The chief took a long pull and set his glass down with a sigh. I waited, but Dehan said, "Chief..."

"Pat."

"Pat, I can't help feeling you have a lot to tell us."

There was a slightly sour twist to his smile when he answered, "Yeah? You think?" He looked away a moment, then started talking, looking at the fire, with the orange light of the flames dancing on his face.

"Anyone who has lived in Belfast, or nearby, has heard of the Brotherhood. But nobody who isn't a member knows anything about them." He glanced at me. "You a Mason?"

"No."

"Lot of cops are Masons. I got no time for secret societies and all that bullshit." He raised an eyebrow at Dehan that bordered on contempt. "I beg your pardon, ma'am."

"The name is Dehan, and I bullshit with the rest of the boys. Your apology is not welcome, Chief."

He nodded once. "Crime is about thirty percent below the national average here in Belfast. They are God-fearing, law-abiding folk. But since 2014, we have seen a steady decrease in violent crime and property crime. And I don't mind telling you that that has exactly nothing to do with the Brotherhood and everything to do with my policing methods."

He looked at us each in turn, as though he was watching to see if his words had registered. When he saw that they had, he went on.

"Talk is, they have a hierarchy, an Elder Brother..."

Dehan said, "Jeremiah."

"That's the word, a council, and then a wider membership."

I pulled a photocopy of Captain Jones' list from my pocket and handed it to him. "Captain Ewan Jones is a member, like his dad before him and apparently his grandfather and so on, back to when the sect was founded. It seems Sally grew up a member of the cult but then broke free. That"—I pointed at the list—"is a list of the people Captain Jones claims are members of the Council."

He picked it up and read it, nodding occasionally. Eventually, he said, "It makes sense." He held it up. "Can I keep this?"

"Sure. Captain Jones stopped short of stating that the Brotherhood had Sally Jones murdered, but his statement implies that it is a distinct possibility."

He sighed heavily and took another long pull on his beer. As he set the glass down, he wiped his mouth with the back of his left hand and asked, "Do you know what an invisible society is?"

Neither of us answered. A shower of spar spat out of the fire, and we all looked at it, like that was more interesting than the question he had just asked us. He searched my face and then Dehan's.

She said, "It sounds like something out of the Da Vinci Code."

He grunted. "I never read it. They told me it was crap. I don't have much time for fiction, Detective Dehan, and I have no time at all for conspiracy theories. But when I took over as chief here, it didn't take me long to discover that there was some kind of vigilante at work. Every year or two, somebody would die. Sometimes it was an accident, sometimes it was a murder, but in every case, it went cold and was filed away." He wagged a finger at her. "After I took over, the crime rate began to fall by a significant percentage, but the number of unexplained deaths did not. It stayed constant. Now, any statistician will tell you that when that happens, it means the cause of those particular deaths is separate and distinct from the others. Because the changes in policing that are reducing violent crime as a whole are not affecting the cause of those particular, unexplained deaths."

He reached in his pocket and pulled out a white envelope. He handed it to me, and I opened it and read it. It was a list of thirteen names. They were all of either Irish or Scottish origin, and each had a date beside it. The dates went back ten years.

"What's this?" I asked, but I knew what the answer would be.

The door opened behind me, and for a moment, I heard the damp hiss of tires on wet asphalt. McFarlane watched over my shoulder till the door closed, then turned back to me. "Those are the unexplained deaths going back ten years. They are spaced no less than six months apart, but no more than twelve. All of those people came from families that had demonstrable links to the Brotherhood..."

Dehan interjected, "What does that mean, exactly?"

"It means there are documented records, either from the parish church, the town hall, or the local newspapers, that the families of these people had at one time belonged to the Brotherhood. Maybe they still do. And every single one of them had strayed from the fold. Either she was living in sin with her boyfriend, or he had taken to the drink, or gambling. One of them was selling drugs and pimping whores..." He stabbed a finger at the paper, punctuating his words. "Every single one of them. Every single one of them had strayed from the Brotherhood's prescribed Warrior's Path."

Dehan frowned. "Warrior's Path?"

He nodded. "Every member of the Brotherhood is a warrior, and is required to live according to the warrior's code, or as they call it, the Warrior's Path. No boozing, no smoking, no drugs, no sex unless it is for procreation, and then only in a sanctified union. The list goes on, you can imagine."

I folded the sheet and slipped it back in the envelope. As I tucked it in my inside pocket, I asked, "So what happened? You started to investigate..."

"I tried, but every line of investigation I opened dried up before I got started. Documents disappeared, parish records vanished inexplicably, the cops I put on it turned up nothing." He sighed and sagged. "They own this town, Stone. Every name on that list you gave me, of the Brotherhood's Council, is in City Hall. Not everyone in City Hall is a member, just like the chief of police isn't, but if you don't play ball, they find a way to bring you down."

"Bring you down, how?"

He pointed at the envelope. "The last name on that list. Sean Butler. He was one detective who was prepared to go up against them. Real Irish firebrand. He had a wife and three kids, and a mortgage he was paying off on his detective's salary and his wife's salary as a teacher.

"A week after he'd started his investigation, two uniforms found an ounce of coke in his desk drawer. Internal Affairs started an investigation. He was suspended without pay for the duration. The bank foreclosed on his mortgage. His kids were expelled from school, and he wound up eating his own .38. He was found in the passenger seat of his truck, down by the river. Nobody thought that was strange."

We fell silent, watching the flames in the fire dance and weave. The waitress came over with our burgers, and Chief McFarlane snarled without looking up, "You're wasting your damned time. She left this town years ago and her family disowned her. I, for one, was glad to see the back of her. We don't need that kind of trash in this town."

The waitress didn't seem to hear and told us to enjoy. As she hurried back to the bar, I spoke quietly. "You need to hand this over to the Feds."

He snapped, "You think I haven't tried? They were oh-so polite in their damned suits but told me there was no evidence for them to proceed upon. Nor was there evidence to suggest that whatever case there might be was within their jurisdiction." He stabbed a finger at me. "You need to take it to the Feds."

I nodded. "If it comes to it, will you testify?"

His face flushed crimson and he shouted, "No! Goddamn it!" Then, in a low, almost inaudible growl, he said, "And I'll tell you something else, Detective, I will not sanction the use of recording equipment to entrap suspects, or to record conversations that were meant to be off the record. Do you understand me?"

"I think so."

"I told Mr. Rose that I would do everything in my power to prevent you from disturbing him at home in his country house. I know there is nothing I can do in law to prevent you from calling on him, but if he calls me and informs me that you are trespassing on his land, I will remove you." He sank back in his chair. "Their church, however, on Miller Street, is a different matter, because it is a charitable institution and open to the general public. He is there every morning at nine, and there is nothing I can do to stop you going there."

We ate in silence for the next ten minutes. When we had finished, he stood abruptly and spoke.

"I have fixed you up at the Belfast Hotel on Main Street. I would like you to be gone by midday tomorrow. You are wasting your time here. We take care of our own business and we do not appreciate the meddling of New Yorkers in our affairs. Accept our hospitality for tonight, and then leave in the morning, please."

There was a handful of people in the pub by now. They all glanced over. A couple of them chuckled and turned back to their drinks. Dehan and I exchanged glances, nodded, sighed, and stood, and Chief McFarlane led the way to the door.

We stepped outside into the damp night. The rain had eased to a light drizzle again, and everything reflected wet light. McFarlane opened his driver's door.

"Get in. I'll drive you to your car."

I got in the passenger seat and Dehan climbed in the back. When we'd slammed the door and he'd pulled onto the road, he reached in his breast pocket and pulled out a burner, which he handed to me.

"It's still recording. My prints, and what I am about to state next, is proof that my intention was to lawfully hand this recording over to Detectives John Stone and Carmen Dehan of the NYPD, in evidence against the Sacred Brotherhood of Christ. I am willing to testify in court against them."

Dehan handed me an evidence bag from the back, and I slipped the phone into it. I glanced at McFarlane. "Thanks."

"My wife is visiting her sister in L.A. But my life is on the line. Get it right and be quick, because I may not last the week."

He dropped us beside the Jag and gave us the address of the hotel where we were booked in. Then we stood and watched him drive away, as his red taillights faded in the night.

ELEVEN

Morning came with broken skies, patches of bright blue in a gray-and-white ceiling of fluff; and beneath it, blue and white clapboard and redbrick houses, washed pristine and set among luminous green lawns and billowing red, ochre, and orange trees.

We stood by the car, speckled with last night's rain. Dehan was on the driver's side, drumming her palms on the roof while I watched her in her fur-lined aviator's jacket and tried to guess what she was going to say. I didn't manage it.

"How does the Mustang tie in?"

"What?"

"You heard me."

I shook my head, then shrugged. "What makes you think it does? And also, what Mustang?"

She sucked her teeth and pursed her lips all at the same time, staring at me across the burgundy roof of the Jag. "The one she was sitting on," she said at last. "With Gus."

I frowned and sighed and shook my head, also all at the same time. "It doesn't, Dehan. The Mustang has nothing to do with our case."

She narrowed her eyes in a way that suggested she was dangerous, unlocked the car, and climbed in. I continued to frown for a moment, then climbed in beside her and slammed the door.

"You want to tell me what's on your mind?"

"Nope."

She fired up the engine, indicated, and pulled out onto the wet blacktop, where we moved west toward the city center at a steady thirty miles per hour.

"Nope?"

"Nope. You know my methods, my dear Watson, apply them."

"This is payback."

"Yup."

"But the difference, my dear Dehan, is that you are not using a method. Your method is that your gut—or some childhood infatuation with Nick Wechsler..."

"Who? And also, it was Johnny Depp in *21 Jump Street*. Not him so much either. It was a '67 Fastback. And also, you are jumping to the conclusion, my dear Stone, that your Holmesian method of logical deduction and analysis is the only method of deduction and analysis. But you are wrong. Intuition, after all"— she turned to look at me with an arched eyebrow—"is no more than the unconscious assimilation, cross-referencing, and analysis of data at a speed which the conscious mind could never hope to match. You..." She pointed at me with her finger. "Use intuitive analysis all the time, but you are not aware of it."

"Dear God, Dehan. I am going to have to forbid you books. What are you becoming?"

"That's not funny."

"Perhaps a little amusing. In any case, if the process of analysis is unconscious, it is of little value to the investigator. You claim a Mustang which you have seen in a photograph is significant..."

"Central."

"Central, even, to our investigation, but you cannot state why. You will have to do a little better than that."

She grunted and spun the wheel into Church Street, then,

after two blocks, spun it again left into Miller Street. She pulled up in front of a large, redbrick building with a tower and a gabled roof, which did not immediately evoke the idea of a church. But a large, brass plaque outside proclaimed it to be the Sacred Brotherhood of Christ. She killed the engine and sat staring at the unassuming blond wood doors with their glass panes.

Suddenly, she turned and squinted at me. "Who did Maya Hernandez say Sally used to hang out with?"

I thought for a moment. "Gus, Ben . . ." I shrugged. "Why, what are you getting at?"

"There was somebody else. A geeky type. Ben called him an Ivy League type."

"Yeah, I remember. So?"

"We should talk to him."

I smiled. "First, we should find him. Meantime, we have found the man who probably ordered her execution. How about we talk to him first?"

She nodded a few times, glanced at the tall, redbrick building, and opened the door.

Through the blond wood doors, we entered a small reception area carpeted in beige, with a white desk, a telephone, and a computer screen. Behind the desk was a young, blond man in his early twenties, dressed in a navy-blue blazer. Behind him, on the wall, was a crucifix that looked more like a sword than a cross. He regarded us with cold eyes and waited.

We showed him our badges, but before we could speak, he said, "I know who you are. I wonder if you do."

Dehan answered, "We may never care. We're here to see Jeremiah Rose."

There was insolence and humor in his eyes. "Do you know that you do the Devil's work?"

I leaned on the desk so my face was close to his and he had to look up to avoid staring into my shirt. "Last time I checked, I was working for the New York Police Department. And the investigation I am conducting is on their behalf. But all it takes is for you to give me one wrong answer and this stops being an NYPD case, I cease to be here as a courtesy of the Belfast PD, and this becomes a federal case. Now, let me ask you a question, kid. Do you know what could happen if this becomes a federal case?"

The humor drained from his face. The insolence stayed, but it was clinging on by its fingernails. He didn't say anything, so I went on.

"It means that if they find proof of conspiracy to murder, everyone involved—and that might include brave little warriors like you—is equally guilty. You ever been inside a high-security jail, kid? Let me tell you, if you're looking for the devil's henchmen, you'll find them in there. Now, cut the crap and tell me where I can find Jeremiah Rose."

His cheeks had turned a bright pink, but he straightened his back and squared his shoulders. "He is expecting you. He's in the Warriors' Prayer Chamber." He pointed to a door beyond the desk. "David will guide you."

I stepped toward the door but turned back when Dehan asked, "He knew we were coming?"

The insolence returned to the kid's face. "If he's expecting you, I guess he must have."

"You got CCTV in this place?"

He shook his smug little head. "We have the eyes of God. They serve us better."

That was all she needed to know. She stepped over to him, took a fistful of his tie, and dragged him to his feet, till his nose was less than an inch from hers.

"Do not look into your enemy's eyes, lest you become your enemy, small fry. I know you. I was reared on stories about you. You have no name, because you are the drones of evil. When the book burning starts, you are in the front line, with the gasoline and the matches, with the glow of the flames in your damned eyes. You're looking for the henchmen of the devil, look in the damned mirror, you little shit!"

She shoved him back in his chair. It overbalanced, and he

sprawled on his back with his legs kicking in the air and the chair casters wedged awkwardly under the desk. I smiled down at him where he lay struggling.

"Shame you didn't get that on CCTV. Still, maybe you can apply for a certified copy from upstairs." I pointed at the ceiling.

We pushed through the door and found ourselves in a terracotta tiled corridor. The walls were whitewashed, and there were two arched doors set in the far wall. On our right, a mahogany staircase carpeted in red ascended to the upper floor. Standing at the foot of that staircase, in a blue blazer and gray pants, was a clone of the kid who was struggling to get to his feet next door. His blond hair was cut short, and his blue eyes watched us without emotion.

"You David?"

"Are you the detectives from New York?"

We showed him our badges. "Detectives Stone and Dehan, NYPD."

"Follow me."

He turned, and we followed him up the stairs. We came to a broad, galleried landing. To the right of the landing was a passage that led to a stained glass window. The doors punctuated the passage on the left.

Directly ahead of us, the wall was bare red brick and rose to some twenty feet or slightly more. Arched double doors stood dead center, and above them a massive, gilded cross, shaped like a sword, hung suspended. Beneath it, on a gilded scroll, were the words "Gladio Christi."

David walked to the door and turned to face us.

"Brother Jeremiah is in prayer. I will tell him you are here."

He didn't wait for an answer. He wasn't asking. He pushed through the double doors, and they swung closed behind him.

I raised an eyebrow at Dehan. "Still worried about that Mustang?"

She eyed me a moment. "How much you reckon this real estate is worth?"

The question surprised me. I thought about it. "I don't know. I'm not familiar with local prices, but a lot."

"What do you think the Council is worth, collectively?"

"Again . . ."

"A lot." She pointed at the cross. "How about that? What do you think that is worth?"

"What are you getting at, Dehan?"

"How about the growing membership?"

"Point?"

"Point: you don't accumulate this kind of wealth by being stupid. You accumulate this kind of wealth by being smart. Executing Gus on the same night as Sally would be stupid. Leaving Ewan Jones as a loose end would be stupid, especially after he had expressed his doubts to the Council. These guys may be as crazy as a soup sandwich, but they are not stupid."

I grunted. I had to agree. "But we can't ignore the circumstantial evidence, plus the testimony we have. Even without forensics, the case is compelling."

She nodded, then stared up at the huge cross. "I know . . ."

The doors opened, and David stepped out. "If you'd care to come through, Brother Jeremiah will see you."

He held the door for us as we stepped through to a Spartan chapel. The walls were whitewashed, and the floor was tiled in oxblood terra-cotta. A central aisle separated twenty-four wooden benches into two blocks of twelve. These faced a plain, stone altar behind which a cross that made no attempt to appear as anything other than a gigantic sword towered thirty feet over the nave.

David allowed the door to swing closed behind us, and his voice echoed high among the rafters.

"The white walls represent the enlightened purity of Christ, to which we aspire, but which we can never reach. The sword represents the burden of our sins, which only He can bear, but also the sword of prophecy."

I turned to look at him. He was smiling at me, but there was a depth of arrogance in his pale eyes.

He went on, "The floor is oxblood, to represent the millions who have died, and the millions who must die, to make His Kingdom a reality."

Dehan curled her lip. "What happened to turning the other cheek and loving your enemies?"

"That is for mankind. But He is the greatest of the avenging angels. Do you know your Bible? Matthew ten thirty-four, 'Do not assume that I have come to bring peace to the Earth; I have not come to bring peace, but a sword.' Thirty-five, 'For I have come to turn a man against his father, a daughter against her mother, a daughter-in-law against her mother-in-law.'"

"Yeah, do you know the context?"

He didn't hesitate. "Yes. The context is the fulfilling of prophecy and the rise of the kingdom of Satan, when our Lord will return upon a crimson charger, and in his hand will he brandish the sword of Divine Justice."

I cut in. "You want to take us to see Jeremiah now?"

"Come right this way."

He led us down the aisle, past the north transept and the chancel to where the apse should be. But instead of the apse, what we came to was a granite wall with an arched, heavy wooden door set in it. He knocked on the door, seemed to count to three, and then turned the handle. He stepped in smartly and held the door for us. "Brother Jeremiah will see you now."

We went through. David closed the door. We were in a circular room with a very high, domed ceiling supported on arches, each of which held an exquisite stained glass window. Together, they seemed to tell the story of Brother Charles McDonnell and his encounter, in Belfast Bay, with Jesus Christ in the form of an avenging angel. The floor was carpeted in burgundy, and at its center there was a large, round table flanked by twelve mahogany chairs upholstered in crimson red. At one of these chairs, at the far end of the table, sat a man.

His age was hard to pin down, but he might have been sixty or seventy years old. He was dressed in a charcoal-gray suit with a burgundy tie. His skin was taut and largely unwrinkled, his hair was white, and his eyes long and pale. He remained immobile, watching us, waiting.

I approached the table and showed him my badge. He didn't look at it. Instead, he looked at my face.

"I am Detective John Stone. This is my partner, Detective Dehan. We are with the New York Police Department."

His voice, when he spoke, was surprisingly high and thin but carried a surprising, arresting authority.

"You have no jurisdiction here, Detective."

"We are operating here in collaboration with the Belfast PD."

His mouth was long, and his lips were thin. His smile was strangely reptilian. "I know whom you are collaborating with, Detective. You are collaborating with Satan. And I am telling you that you have no jurisdiction here."

I felt Dehan's hand on my shoulder, a slight squeeze, and she pulled out a chair opposite Brother Jeremiah and sat.

"Let's cut the bullshit, Jeremiah. I'm getting bored of all this crap. You are running a nonprofit organization in the state of Maine, and you and your organization come under state and federal law, just like every other mother's son in this country. And if you are a person of interest in an investigation, you are going to answer our damned questions, either here or in a police station, just like everybody else."

His eyes were hooded as he listened, and there was no mistaking the rage behind them.

"Detective Dehan, that's a Jew name, isn't it?"

"Yeah, as Jewish as Jesus of Nazareth."

His face flinched. "Let me explain something to you, Dehan, this is the Sacred home of Jesus, not Jesus the bringer of peace, but Jesus the warrior. And you who seek to defile Him, or come here as the henchmen of the Devil, come here at your own peril."

"Is that a threat?"

He shook his head once, slowly. "No, we are God-fearing, law-abiding folk in this town. I seek merely to advise you that the wrath of God, when it strikes, is a fearsome and terrible thing. And you would be well advised to leave this place, while you still can."

TWELVE

I pulled up a chair next to Dehan's and sat.

"Thanks for the advice. Now, are you prepared to answer some questions or not?"

He offered me his reptilian smile and licked his thin lips with the tip of his tongue. "Well, that kind of depends on the question, Detective Stone."

"Where are the other members of the Council?"

"I am not in a position to answer that question."

Dehan cut in, "So perhaps you can tell us who the members of the Council are."

A small laugh. "I am so sorry, Detective. I am not in a position to give you that information. It is strictly confidential."

I gave a single nod. "Tell me, does the Council still convene for Hearings of Sentence of Death and Decrees of Execution?"

The smile faded. The tip of his tongue darted across the slit of his mouth. "Where did you hear about that?"

"Answer the question please, Mr. Rose."

"I am not in a position . . ." He faltered. "Who told you . . . ? Where . . . ?"

"It is a matter of public record that the Brotherhood never abolished either. But equally it was understood that they de facto stopped convening for hearings on both matters. It is understood that the Council has not issued a death sentence or a Decree of Execution for well over a century, perhaps two. Now I am asking you if that is correct, or whether the Council have continued to issue and execute death sentences, or indeed started to do so again in the recent past."

He hesitated for a second. "I cannot answer that question."

Dehan snapped, "What is preventing you from answering that question?"

"The affairs of the Council of the Sacred Brotherhood of Christ are strictly confidential."

"There is no confidentiality where murder is concerned. If the Council of the Brotherhood are issuing sentences of death and orders of execution, then that is murder under federal law, and aiding, abetting, and conspiring in that murder is itself murder. Now quit stalling and answer the damned question! Is the Council of the Sacred Brotherhood of Christ issuing sentences of death and orders to execute those sentences? Yes or no?"

His reaction was violent and startling. His face flushed. He slammed the palm of his hand down hard on the table. The noise was loud and echoed around the chamber. Then his voice came like the shrill scream of a parrot. "You have no jurisdiction here! This is the house of Christ!"

I let the echo die, then spoke quietly. "Answer here, now. Or you can answer in an interrogation room, here or in New York. You choose. Either way, you will answer."

He leaned forward. His eyes narrowed, and again his small tongue darted out and flicked over his lips. "The Council no longer convenes for Hearings of Sentence of Death, nor Decrees of Execution. It hasn't done so for over a hundred years."

It was practically verbatim what Captain Ewan Jones had said, and it now sounded rehearsed, like a stock reply.

"But they were never abolished."

He sat back, his eyes narrowed, his mouth no more than a scar on his face. "They were never abolished."

"Because they wanted to keep their options open for the future."

"You might think so. I could not possibly comment."

"Brother Jeremiah, as Jesus Christ is your witness, did you, sitting in council, sentence Sally Jones to death?"

He sneered. "As the Lord Jesus Christ is my witness, I did not, sitting in council, sentence Sally Jones to death."

"Did you issue an order of execution against her?"

"No, I did not."

"Did anybody else, acting on behalf of the Council, or the Brotherhood, issue any such order of execution?"

"I cannot answer that question."

I sighed. "We have sworn testimony that shortly before her death, you sent both Captain Ewan Jones and two other men to speak to both Sally Jones and Angus McBride, a young man she was involved with."

"Another henchman of Satan. But, as far as I am aware, Detective, there is no law against sending a messenger to a lost soul to beg her, or him, to return to the righteous path."

Dehan answered. "But there is a law against sending a messenger to murder those people who stray from the path."

"To act according to God's will is no sin. And to execute a deviant according to God's will is not murder."

I asked him, "And was it God's will that Sally Jones should die that night?"

He smiled his lizard smile again and flicked his tongue. "Clearly, it was."

"And did you act on his will and bring about her death?"

His smile deepened. "I have already told you I did not. It seems to me, Detective, that we are going in circles."

"Will you give us the names of the men you sent to visit Sally and Angus?"

"I am sorry, Detective, I cannot give you that information."

I sank back in my chair. "I am not sure that you fully understand this situation, Mr. Rose, or this process."

"What process exactly, Detective Stone?"

I pointed at him. "You continue to stonewall us, and we take the evidence and the testimony we have and we hand it over to the Federal Bureau of Investigation. We are guests of the Belfast PD, so our powers are limited here. The FBI will have no such limitations, and they will take you and your brotherhood apart piece by piece and they will find every skeleton you have in your cupboard. They will find the skeletons of the mice the Brotherhood cat killed back in 1649. They will not stop until they have explained every unexplained death that has occurred over the last ten years."

His face drained to a pasty white, then slowly flushed an angry red. "Do your worst. You will not intimidate me. You can bring the hosts of Satan to my door, but you will not strike fear into our hearts. We are the chosen warriors of Christ, and we shall continue to do His work, whatever the consequences!"

Dehan sighed. "What are you saying, Rose? That's a lot of hot air, a lot of words, but what does it mean? You got the balls to come out and say, 'We are going to continue to execute those who transgress against God's law'?" She stood and leaned forward on the table, pointing at him. "For all your talk of God, and how you are doing His work, are you man enough to stand up and say, 'Yes! We have executed whores, and deviants, and blasphemers, and harlots!' Are you courageous enough to speak the truth in God's name? Or are you just a cringing, whining gasbag who hides behind the cross because he is too much of a coward to stand up to his enemies?"

He stood by degrees. He was trembling. David moved quickly and silently across the room to his side, but Jeremiah pushed him aside.

"I will not be insulted in my own church by a Jewess!" He spat the word out. "And I will not be interrogated by heathens and servants of Satan! We have done God's work, and I am proud of the work we have done. But you will get not a word out of me, for we of the Brotherhood are sworn to secrecy." He waved a finger at Dehan, and suddenly his age was visible in his face and in his movements. "But you may be sure, you daughter of Babylon, that those who have died at the hands of the Brotherhood deserved to die, and be sure that if you come against Christ or his warriors, you will be met by such a force that you have not dreamt of!"

I spoke quietly. "Threatening a police officer is an offense, Mr. Rose."

"Consider it not a threat, but a warning against defying Divine Law."

I stood. "Don't leave town, Mr. Rose. We may need to talk to you again. In fact, I am sure we will. Next time, the surroundings won't be so divine."

We pushed out the double doors in silence. On the stairs on the way down, we passed a man in a well-cut suit with well-cut hair. He glanced at us with curious eyes and muttered, "Good morning," then hurried on up.

When we stepped back into the reception, the young kid was back in his chair. He looked at us resentfully and I asked him, "Who's the guy in the suit?"

He curled his lip and sneered like he'd scored a point in some obscure game.

"The mayor."

I sighed. "Outstanding."

Outside, a steady yet listless downpour had started. It was a steady hiss of rain backed by a timpani of clatters and wet clinks from overflowing gutters where the water was slapping at front yards and backyards and iron grates: the steady wet patter of October in the Bronx. I stood a moment under the small porch and pulled up my collar. Dehan shuddered beside me and held my arm with both of hers.

A red car with its headlamps reflecting on the wet blacktop sighed past, like it was depressed it had its lights on so early in the morning. We both looked up at the sky. It was no more reassuring than the sodden asphalt in front of us. I held out my hand. "Give me the keys, I'll open the door."

"You were born in the wrong age, Stone. You belong at the round table with King Arthur."

She handed me the keys, and I loped across the puddles that had formed in the gravel driveway.

In the muffled silence of the car, as we pulled out back onto Miller Street, she said, "So now what?"

"Coffee."

"Yeah, cool, now do you mind answering the question?"

"I do, and you know why."

I turned left onto High Street and then took another left onto Beaver Street.

"Because for the first time in your career, you are stumped and don't know who dunnit."

I shrugged. "That's putting it a little strong, Dehan. I know who dunnit, and I even know how it was done. Where I am stumped is in proving it."

We passed a cute row of old-world, redbrick shops and turned into a cobbled yard beside the Moonbat City Baking Company, a tall, stand-alone redbrick with a gabled roof, that served coffee and cakes all day long.

We chose a couple of muffins and some black coffee and sat at a sash window looking out at the New England rain soaking the green banks opposite and washing the mural on the wall of the SS *Belfast*. The Moonbat was quiet and dark in the poor, rainy light. Dehan spoke quietly.

"So your theory is that Jeremiah Rose has been on a ten-year murder spree, using his—to borrow one of his words—henchmen to carry out the hits."

I pulled the list of suspected victims that Chief McFarlane had given me from my inside pocket and handed it to her. "The first name on that list was shot with a nine-millimeter pistol six months after Jeremiah Rose took office."

She raised her eyebrows at me. "How do you know that?"

"I couldn't sleep last night. So while you were gently snoring, I did some homework on my laptop." A comely waitress brought us a tray laden with coffee and cake and bid us enjoy. As she retreated back to the counter, I broke my muffin in two. "People like Jeremiah don't get that way spontaneously. They are years in the making. In Jeremiah's case, his family have been members since the cult was formed, in 1649. He was reared a Brother from the day he was born, and my guess is that he has been fanatical about the mission of the Brotherhood since he was a young teen." I pointed at the list and spoke with my mouth full. "And as soon as he was elected to high office, he reactivated the Sentence of Death and Decrees of Execution, and took out his first victim."

She shook her head, broke her muffin in four, and dunked one of the sections in her coffee, then stuffed the sagging, saturated cake in her mouth and grinned. "Mh-mh." She shook her head again. "This time," she said after she had swallowed, "you have failed to turn left at Albuquerque."

"I did what?"

"Bugs Bunny. Think about it, Sensei. If you are right, for about twenty years these guys have been pulling off hits against servants of the Devil, and they have been doing it so well nobody has ever been able to trace the hits back to them. And then, suddenly, they make the glaring mistake of hitting both Gus and Sally on the same night. I don't buy it. Also, none of these cases . . ."—she waved the list at me—"involves mutilation of the body."

I sighed. "I know, that troubles me too."

She stuck another piece of cake in her mouth and chewed methodically. Then she wagged a finger at me as she reached for her cup. "I am not saying that Sally was not on Jeremiah's hit list. Maybe she was. But I am saying that it doesn't make sense that he killed her."

I thought about it and shook my own head back at her. "No, Ritoo Glasshopper, what you are saying is that you can't see the sense. That is a different matter."

She frowned and raised an eyebrow at the same time, which is not easy to do. "You need to explain that."

"All that is needed is for Jeremiah to have a special reason for killing Sally. And that special reason boils down to some kind of special relationship. And if their families were at all close, which is not unlikely, then we have the potential for that relationship."

She sighed. "I'm beginning to sound like you, but that is a lot of ifs. And if you are right, and if we could prove it, it is simply circumstantial."

"I know." I sighed. "I hate to admit it, Dehan, but we are getting very close to the point where we need to hand this over to the bureau. But before we do that, I want to talk to Captain Jones one more time. I am pretty sure he hasn't told us everything."

She stared at me awhile. "We need to get back to the Bronx. There is something I want to look into."

I smiled at her. "You cutting me out?"

She shook her head. "I am doing a Stone. You disagree with my theory, so I am going to pursue it my way without telling you what I am doing."

"I get it. It's payback." I blended a sigh with a smile and offered it to her. She smiled back. I said, "Okay, we'll see if Jones is back or if he's still in New York. If he's here, we talk to him, then we go back and talk to the chief, and you can look into your theory. Work for you?"

"Yup."

I pulled out my phone and called Captain Jones. He didn't answer.

THIRTEEN

I tried his landline and then I tried his cell. I got his answering service on both and asked him to get back to us. While I searched for his address, Dehan went to the wholesome waitress and asked her if she knew where Captain Ewan Jones lived. She said, well, sure she did, and gave us his address on Cedar Street.

It was less than half a mile's drive, down Main Street and left into Cedar. His house was the sixth on the left, a vast, L-shaped, white clapboard building with a gray slate roof. The door was under a Palladian porch supported on pillars, and in the crook of the L, there was a neat lawn with an ash tree at its center. The rain had eased while we had been breaking our fast, and now, as I climbed out of the Jag, I could see small drops of rain falling, desultorily, from the leaves.

We crossed the wet asphalt and climbed the three steps to the door. Dehan knocked, then rang the bell. After a couple of minutes, she did it again, and across the lawn, maybe thirty feet away, I saw a drape move, and a couple of minutes after that, the door opened and a large woman with a round face looked out at us like we were an annoying glitch in her system.

"Yes?" I showed her my badge and drew breath, but she cut in, "That's a New York badge. This is Maine."

I smiled at her. "I know where I am, but thanks anyhow. I am Detective John Stone; this is my partner, Detective Carmen Dehan. We would like to see Captain Jones. Is he at home?"

A small frown, and her eyes narrowed. "He ain't here."

"Can you tell us where he is, or when he is likely to be back?"

She shifted her weight and planted her fist on her hip.

"Well, as I understood it, he was in New York talking to the police. So I am just wondering why the New York police are here, seeking to talk to him."

Dehan answered. "We did speak to him at the station, Ms. . . . ?"

"Mrs. Davis."

"Mrs. Davis, we spoke to Captain Jones in New York, and we are here on the strength of what he told us. We just need to talk to him again. Have you any idea when he will be back?"

She arched an eyebrow. "I am not my brother's keeper, Detective. Why don't you call him and ask him?"

"I have, but he does not answer his telephone."

"Then I can help you no further."

She closed the door and left us staring at the high-gloss wood.

Dehan skipped down the steps and made her way back to the car while I called the chief.

"Inspector John Newman."

"Chief, it's Detective Stone . . ."

"Ah, John. I have been anxious to hear from you. How is it going?"

"Complicated."

"Of all the possible answers, that was the one . . ."

"Yeah, I know. We need to discuss this with you. I'm beginning to feel it's time to hand it over to the Feds. Dehan doesn't agree and feels we need to explore another avenue."

"I see, but you don't favor this avenue . . . ?"

I had reached the car, and Dehan had her ass planted on the

hood, watching me with her arms crossed. I sighed. "That would be putting it too strongly, sir. Let's just say that Detective Dehan has more faith in it than I have."

"John, we have spoken about this, and you know that I should like you to, indeed, as you always do, leave no stone unturned before handing it over. This is, like it or not, a showcase for the work you are doing, and a successful conclusion is important to the department."

I nodded, as though he could see me. "Yes, sir. I understand. We'll be there first thing in the morning, and I'll brief you on the progress so far."

I hung up, and Dehan and I stared at each other for a moment. Then she voiced my thoughts. "Should we tell the chief we're leaving? It seems like the courteous thing to do, but . . ." She shrugged. "Maybe give him a call?"

I shook my head. "No, let them see us in retreat."

We went back to the hotel and spent half an hour settling our bill and packing our bags. When we'd thrown them in the trunk, we made our way back, one more time, toward the station house, a quarter of a mile down the same road. As we drove, the rain, which had largely held off for the last hour, began to come down. It wasn't torrential, but it was steady, and on the sidewalk, people were opening their umbrellas, or running for cover, pulling up their collars.

I flipped on the wipers, and they began their squeak and thud as the world fractured into wet, broken pieces and was then swept away to reveal oily patterns of light on the blacktop under a dark, wet sky. The trees at the roadside tossed and bowed under the downpour, and the tall, narrow, redbrick buildings, with their gabled roofs, seemed to stand sentinel over a wet, gray world.

One thing you don't often see is police cars and ambulances ranged outside station houses. That's because station houses are not usually the scene of crimes. So it took me a moment to register that the liquid red-and-blue lights I was seeing smeared across the windshield were the lights of an ambulance and a couple of patrols ranged around the door of the station house. I glanced at Dehan.

She was scowling and returned my glance. "What the hell . . . ?"

"McFarlane . . ."

Dehan was shaking her head. "No, it's too much. It's too much, Stone . . ."

I pulled up behind the nearest prowler and we climbed out. Police tape had been strung around the entrance, and there were uniforms standing about, holding back a small crowd. I could see an ambulance and what I assumed to be the ME's car and a crime scene van. As we approached the cordon, a big sergeant stepped up, observing us with hostile eyes.

"You can't come through. This is a crime scene."

I showed him my badge. "Detectives Stone and Dehan, NYPD, we're here at the invitation of Chief McFarlane. What has happened here?"

He didn't answer for a moment, then turned and called to a uniform on the door. "Hey! O'Brien! Tell Detective Connors the two New York cops are here." He turned back and looked at us. "You better come through. He wants to talk to you."

He raised the tape, and we ducked under. Dehan stared into his face. "What happened?"

"You better talk to the detective."

I snapped, "Quit stalling! Where is Chief McFarlane?"

The big sergeant observed me with cold eyes and gave his head a small shake. "You don't get to throw your weight around here, Detective. This ain't New York, and here you ain't shit. Talk to Detective Connors." He jerked his head toward the door. "Inside. He has some questions for you."

We made our way to the door and stepped through to the front desk. There were a lot of cops. More than you would normally see in a station house, because most cops work out on the streets. In that moment, it looked like the whole of Belfast PD was on-site. The desk sergeant glanced at us.

"You the New York cops?"

I approached. "Yeah. Where's the chief? What's happened here?"

"Detective Connors is on his way down. Just wait here."

We didn't have to wait long. The door opened, and a big, athletic guy in his early fifties leaned out. He glanced at us both and seemed to growl. "Stone and Dehan?"

We told him we were, and he jerked his head at us. "Come on up. I need to talk to you."

We followed him up the stairs among a chaos of cops. On the upper floor, I caught a glimpse of the chief's office. It was packed with people, but before I could have a good look, Connors was ushering us into another office with his name on the door. He closed it behind us and gestured us toward two chairs at a melamine desk. He lowered himself carefully into a large leather chair on the other side and took a moment to consider us.

Before he could speak, I said, "Where is Chief McFarlane?"

The corner of his mouth twitched. "Why?"

"Because we need to talk to him?"

"What do you want to talk to him about?"

I frowned. "That is between him and us. I don't see how that is any of your concern."

"You don't?"

"I just told you I don't."

He picked up a pencil, examined it like he wasn't sure it was a pencil, and sank back in his chair, holding it in both hands. He eyed Dehan and then me by turns, trying to decide whom to ask. He settled on Dehan.

"When was the last time you saw Chief McFarlane?"

My patience was wearing thin, but Dehan's was already out. "What's happened to him?"

"Who says anything has happened to him?"

"Come on, Connors! Do we look like rookies to you? You got tape across the damned station house. The place is crawling with cops, there is an ambulance and a crime scene van downstairs!

Now you're asking us about why we were meeting your chief. How stupid do you think we are?"

He raised an eyebrow at her. "I haven't made up my mind. Now do you want to answer the damned question, or do I need to take you in as material witnesses?"

I spoke up. "The Forty-Third has an agreement with Belfast PD to cooperate on an investigation we are conducting. We met with Chief McFarlane yesterday evening. We went to Darby's and had a beer and a burger. He wasn't all that cooperative, and we hit a dead end. We were here to thank him for his help and be on our way. Now I have answered your question, you want to answer ours? What's happened to him?"

He focused his eyes on the pencil and nodded at it for a while. Maybe he'd finally realized it was a pencil.

"What was the nature of your case?"

"You're crossing a line and you know it."

He raised his eyes to meet mine. "Chief McFarlane has been murdered in his own office. The killer came in, walked past all the cops in the building, went into the chief's office unchallenged, shot him in the heart, and left undetected. Nobody saw him, nobody heard him. So if I am crossing a line, Detective, I don't really give a damn. Because I intend to find who killed Pat and make them pay to the full extent of the law. Now, you can answer my damned question, or I can pull you in. You choose."

I glanced at Dehan. A sudden gust of wind splattered rain against the window and outside, the trees bowed under a leaden sky. I thought for a moment and decided I had nothing to lose.

"I head up a cold-case unit at the Forty-Third. We're investigating a case from October 2010. Sally Jones was murdered in the Bronx. Her family was from Belfast, and they were members of the Brotherhood..."

I paused to watch his reaction. His pupils contracted, the muscles at the corners of his eyes tensed. Other than that, there was no reaction, and that in itself was significant.

I said, "You know the Brotherhood?"

"Everyone in Belfast knows the Brotherhood. You must know that by now. So what happened?"

"My chief talked to your chief, and he agreed to cooperate. We talked, and he advised us that the Brotherhood were just a private, exclusive club of people who carried a lot of weight in the community. He didn't want to ruffle feathers, and basically he'd be grateful if we went home as soon as possible." I sighed and spread my hands. "He told us Jeremiah Rose would be at church in the morning and asked us to refrain from bothering him. We told him that wasn't going to happen and we needed to talk to him, which we did this morning. It was a waste of time."

"So her family were involved in the Brotherhood. A lot of families in Belfast have ties to the Brotherhood. What makes you think they have something to do with your investigation?"

I snorted a short laugh and shook my head. "Give me a good reason why I should make you privy to that."

"Because I am investigating his death, and your investigation might have something to do with it. Also, right now, I am still waiting for confirmation from the Forty-Third that you are who you say you are."

Out of the corner of my eye, I saw Dehan turn and look at me. She had her chin on her fist and one eyebrow raised. I sighed, like he was twisting my arm.

"From information received, we believed that Sally Jones had been visited by members of the Brotherhood a few days before her death. A witness also informed us that a man fitting Captain Ewan Jones' description had visited her on a couple of occasions shortly before her death. From our background investigations, we understood that the Brotherhood had a history of punishing and executing members who had strayed from the righteous path. It seemed a slim lead, but it was one we had to follow up, especially as we had information that the Rose family and the Jones family were very close."

It was a long shot, but it was worth taking, and it paid dividends. He was motionless for a long moment, then smiled.

"It wasn't a slim lead, Stone, you were clutching at straws. We are aware of that case here. Sally was one of our own, and the Jones family is highly respected in Belfast. They were one of the founding families in this town, and also of the Sacred Brotherhood of Christ. When Sally died, it hit us all hard. But I am afraid you are on a wild goose chase. The Brotherhood started out three hundred years ago as Christ's warriors, but times have changed, and they haven't been involved in that kind of nonsense for two hundred years. The fact that the Rose family and the Jones are joined by marriage and have business interests in common simply reflects the close nature of our community. This is New England, not New York. The idea that the Rose family or the Jones could be involved in a homicide is absurd."

He offered us a small, humorless laugh and looked at Dehan. "Forgive me for being blunt, but we have one of the lowest crime rates in the country, and we are made up of small, tightly knit communities. Sally moved to an overcrowded metropolis which is notorious for its crime rate, and once there, chose to get involved in a very dangerous world of drugs, alcohol, and possibly prostitution. To look for your killer here is absurd. You need to go back home."

I nodded, then shrugged. "Sure, that makes a lot of sense . . ." I pointed at his door. "But I hope the irony isn't lost on you that we are having this conversation because your chief just got murdered in his own office."

His eyes were as cold and hard as pack ice. "It's not lost on me, Detective, that he died during the visit of two Bronx detectives to our town."

Dehan was quick to react. "Are you accusing us of homicide, Detective Connors? I hope you have more to back that up than the simple fact that we are New Yorkers."

"I am not accusing you of anything, Detective Dehan." He said it, but his tone and the look in his eyes said that he wanted to. "I am just observing the irony, like your partner here. I would ask you to make yourselves available for the coroner's hearing and for any possible questions we may have for you. In the meantime, I would be grateful if you returned to your own jurisdiction as soon as you are able."

"We just came to thank Chief McFarlane for his help and hospitality. We have nothing left to do in Belfast. I hope you catch the bastard who did this. I liked McFarlane. I thought he was one of the good guys."

He watched us leave but didn't answer. By the time we got outside, the rain had eased back to a drizzle, and Chief McFarlane's body, covered in a blanket, was being loaded into the ambulance. We raised our collars and made our way back to the car in silence, across the wet reflections of the pulsing red-and-blue lights on the blacktop.

FOURTEEN

We got back to the Bronx at about six p.m. On the way, Dehan had persuaded me to pass by the Waddling Duck. I had asked her what for, but all she did was smile and say, "Allow me my small, intellectual vanity, my dear Stone."

The same clouds that had been drizzling over Maine were now bellying down over New York, rolling in off the Atlantic and discharging their load in a steady downpour. We crawled down Westchester Avenue in the failing light, with the hunched, sodden crowds milling past along the sidewalks and the cars and trucks stopping and starting in the late rush-hour traffic.

On the far side of the road, I saw the sign for the Waddling Duck over the graffiti-covered steel blind. Parked out front was a locksmith's van, and in front of it a patrol car. Dehan pointed and said, "Cut across and park behind the van."

I glanced at her. "What?"

"Do it, big guy. I won't be long, I just need to do a couple of things."

I slowed, indicating left, and earned myself a few honks and choice epithets of the New York variety. Finally, I made it across the road and pulled into a space behind the locksmith's van. Dehan pulled up her collar, climbed out, and ran the few paces to the prowler. I saw the window slide down, and she spoke a few words before the door opened and a uniformed cop climbed out. At the same time, the driver's door of the van opened too, and a guy in blue overalls got out. All three of them went over to the steel blind, and the guy in overalls hunkered down to work on the padlock. By that time, I had got out too and joined Dehan under the awning. She ignored me.

"Dehan, you want to tell me what's going on?"

She gave me a sweet smile. "Sure."

I waited, but she looked at the uniformed cop beside her, who was pulling an envelope from his pocket. He handed it to her, and she thanked him. She took a document from the envelope and scanned it, turning slightly so I couldn't see what it was. When she was done, she put it back in the envelope and nodded at the cop.

"That's great. We can take it from here."

He nodded and returned to his car. As the door slammed, the lock popped, and the locksmith hauled up the roller blind, revealing a black, arched door and beside it a smoked glass window. The locksmith went to work on the door.

I said, "Dehan?"

She turned to face me and placed one long finger on my chest. "Annoying, ain't it?"

"A little, yes."

She closed her left eye and grinned malevolently. "Suck it up, buster!"

"Okay, Detective, the door is open and you can go in. You want I should fix the lock so you can close it up again when you leave?"

Dehan turned away from me. "Yup," she said. "That's the idea." And she stepped inside, pulling her cell from her pocket to use as a flashlight. I followed her into the musty darkness of the bar. In the beam from her phone, I saw the lugubrious shadows of upended chairs stacked on tables. The far end of the room was in deep shadow, but at the front, a long bar occupied the middle of the floor. There were still bottles, half-full or half-empty, stacked along the dark shelves. Dehan paced slowly around the room, illuminating the corners and the alcoves, then allowing them to plunge back into shadow.

"At least tell me what you're looking for."

"I can't."

"Why not?"

She stopped and flashed the light in my face. "You mean what is it that is stopping me from telling you? You want to be careful with those open questions, Stone. Try to focus them more closely."

"Okay, you made your point. Now you're being a pain in the ass. What is it that is preventing you from telling me what you are looking for? Satisfied?"

"I can't tell you, because I am not entirely sure." Her steps brought her close to the bar, and she played the light slowly across the shelves and the surface where the till was. There were still order and receipt pads, a glass with a few pens and pencils in it, and some rubber bands, a mug, a corkscrew, and a small teddy bear. All the paraphernalia that people tend to accumulate when they spend over eight hours a day in the same place.

"I used to hang out in bars like this one when I was younger. I know the kind of atmosphere that builds up in places like this. You make friendships that are deep, though not lasting . . ."

Her voice trailed off and she stopped moving.

"You used to hang out in a bar like this?"

"Briefly."

"Huh . . ."

"Long story. Some other time. But they always tended to have . . . Hold this."

She handed me her cell. I took hold of it, and she pulled on some latex gloves and vaulted the bar. Now I approached and saw that she was looking at a series of photographs and postcards stuck to a board beside the till and beneath the drinks. She smiled and finished her sentence. ". . . one of these."

I leaned on the bar and focused the light on the board. There were maybe two dozen pictures and a handful of postcards, mainly from tropical locations. Dehan reached back her hand without looking at me. "Give me the phone, big guy."

I put it in her hand, and she started working her way through the photographs. From where I was standing, I could see several that showed a band playing and a mass of heaving bodies against a dark background. Others were close-ups of several people with their arms around each other, staring into the camera, laughing and making faces.

Suddenly, she stopped. Her cell was illuminating a picture of Gus and Sally, and a couple of other guys. She unpinned it and put it into an evidence bag, then continued along the rows of pictures. I felt a strange stab of excitement as I watched.

A moment later, she stopped again. There was Gus, and Sally laughing into the camera, with a third guy. I recognized him from the first picture. He was young, clean cut, and had that Ivy League look. He was nothing like Sally and Gus and looked strangely out of place, but he was grinning and looked happy to be there.

She took down that picture too, and soon found a couple more. Each one went into an evidence bag, and she set them out on the counter in front of me. "Maybe you should have spent more time in bars when you were younger, Stone, and less time at the chess club."

"That's funny. My sides are aching."

She ignored me. "You reckon this is our Ivy League guy? The nerd?"

"Seems likely, but how does this help?"

She shrugged. "I don't know. But I figure if all the guys and gals that were there, who we have spoken to, don't know what happened, then maybe the one guy who was there, who nobody spoke to, might have something useful to tell us."

I frowned at her. "Dehan, Sally was executed by the Brotherhood. Chief McFarlane was executed for helping us in the investigation. Jeremiah Rose all but confessed, and we have the proof that the two families were close. Sally was an affront to everything the two families stood for. Why are you still looking for another explanation? We need to hand this over to the bureau and let them finish the job. It's that simple."

She smiled and shook her head in the dim glow of her flashlight. "No, you are overlooking something."

"So enlighten me! What am I overlooking?"

"The Mustang."

I sighed. "Come on, Dehan! What makes you think that Mustang has any connection at all with this case? Gus must have worked on a dozen Mustangs in his time."

"Maybe, but I don't think so."

"Why?"

"You mean what makes me think not?"

"Yes, Dehan. That is what I mean."

"You weren't really interested in that photograph, Stone, so you didn't really look closely. Also, you're more of a car guy than a bike guy. But if you had looked closely, you would have noticed a couple of things."

"Like what?"

"Like the fact that, in the background, you can see that his workshop is full of bikes, and parked outside are bikes. The only car in the picture—in the whole vicinity of his workshop—is the Mustang."

I sighed. "Okay, maybe he didn't work on dozens of Mustangs. But what does that tell us?"

"That the Mustang was special."

"Okay, so . . . ?"

"So did you look at the license plate?"

I sighed, then smiled and laughed. "No, Dehan, I did not."

She winked. "Ya shoulda, big guy. Ya shoulda."

"You going to tell me why?"

"Nope. I need to confirm one or two things. And if I am right, you gonna git down on your knees, brother, and weep!"

"Nice."

"You betcha."

"I am figuring the paper the uniform gave you was a court order."

She nodded. "I called the chief and had him arrange it for me."

"While I was gently snoring?"

"While you were gently snoring, partner."

She vaulted the bar again, and we made our way back out to the sidewalk, where the locksmith was finishing up. He closed the place up again and handed Dehan the keys.

We climbed back in the Jag, and I fired up the engine. I paused a moment before putting it in gear and put a smile on the right side of my face, where it looks gently ironic.

"Now what?"

"Now I want these pictures run through facial recognition. I have some other ideas, which I won't tell you about until I have explored them a little further." I drew breath, but she raised a finger. "Don't even dream about complaining."

I pulled out into the stream of traffic. As we turned onto White Plains, I said, "Did I mention you are being a supreme pain in the ass?"

"No, but I kind of got it anyway."

"Oh, good."

"I'll make you moussaka tonight to make up for it."

I sucked my teeth and shook my head. "Moussaka may not be enough. It may require more than that . . ."

She made a guttural chuckling sound that was almost disturbing. "I'll see what I can do."

I PARKED the Jag outside the station house and headed up the stairs for the inspector's office. At the door to the detectives' room, Dehan paused and looked in.

"I'll see you up there."

"You'll what?"

"Go on up. I'll be there in five."

"Where are you going?"

She touched her nose with her finger and winked. "Indulge my . . ."

"Little intellectual vanity, yeah, I remember."

She disappeared into the detectives' room, and I climbed the stairs to the chief's office.

"Ah, Stone, come in. Where is Carmen?"

"Indulging her intellectual vanity."

"Oh." He nodded. "Good. Sit, please." I lowered myself into a chair across from him at his desk. He smiled at me. "Will she be joining us?"

"She's on her way up. She's looking into something."

He raised his eyebrows in inquiry.

"I don't know what, sir. She is pursuing a different line in this investigation and seems reluctant to share her thoughts with me."

He chuckled comfortably. "Payback." Then he frowned. "I am fielding a lot of questions at the moment, John. A number of papers want to know what case you are working on, and how it is progressing. They want to follow up on the press conference. We have several agents who want to represent you and believe they can spin a reality TV show." He hesitated, then made an effort at a grin that looked more like regretful distaste. "I'm afraid Carmen is worth considerably more than you, as a TV personality, not, obviously . . ." He waved his hand about.

"I understand, sir."

"So you see, we do need a speedy and successful . . ." He trailed off and sighed.

I echoed his sigh. "Sir, what happened in this case is very clear. I know who killed Sally Jones, I know why, and I know how, but what is missing is the concrete evidence, the physical proof."

He sagged back in his chair. "John, I have to say it was a regrettable choice, just at this time . . ."

I ignored the comment. "In any case, sir, I do think this is one for the bureau. We are looking at multiple murders spanning at least two states, and conducted by a religious organization . . ."

"Oh, lord . . ."

"We haven't the resources to conduct the investigation, and frankly, I don't think we have the pull to get the warrants we need. The cult in question seems to include most of the pillars of Belfast society."

There was a knock at the door, and Dehan came in, looking smug. The chief smiled at her and gestured to a chair beside mine. "Carmen, do you agree with John that this is a case for the bureau?"

She sat and frowned to cover her smile. "Up to a point, sir."

"Up to a point." He smiled and blinked. "I think you had better explain."

"You see, sir, I think we have two, possibly three, separate crimes here. There is a loose connection, but they are separate and distinct."

I scratched my chin, and the chief sank back in his chair and ran his fingers through his hair.

"Two, or possibly three . . ."

"That's why it has been so hard to crack. You see, I think in Maine, we have a series of murders conducted at the orders of the Brotherhood . . ."

"The Brotherhood . . ."

She glanced at me. "You didn't explain? The Sacred Brotherhood of Christ, a religious sect sworn to act as the sword of Christ and strike down the servants of Satan. Apparently, they stopped doing that about two hundred years ago, but, and I do agree with Stone on this, in the last twenty years, when the current Elder Brother took office, it seems he reinstituted the trials and executions."

"You have some concrete evidence for this?"

I pulled Chief McFarlane's cell from my pocket and placed it on the desk. "Some circumstantial evidence, which could be ruled hearsay."

I pressed play, and we sat through McFarlane's exposition of his case. When it was finished, I also pulled out the list of possible victims he had drawn up, and Captain Jones' list of Council members.

"It is a very tight-knit community, and the Jones and the Rose families are bound by both business and marriage. It looks very much as though Chief Pat McFarlane was in fact onto something, and people who strayed badly from the fold were—and are—being executed." I paused and sighed. "This morning, somebody walked into his office, in broad daylight, at the station house, and shot him through the heart."

He was very still for a moment. "Dear God . . ." He turned to Dehan. "But you believe . . ."

She shook her head once and cut him short. "That is one set of homicides. The link with Sally is through her brother. But Gus and Sally are separate, and I don't believe they were murdered by the Brotherhood."

He turned to me. "John?"

I spread my hands. "I believe they were, sir."

"Carmen, on the face of it, it would seem self-evident. What reason have you for believing they are separate?"

"For a start, killing Gus and Sally on the same night within a few hours of each other is uncharacteristically sloppy. These guys have been getting away with murder for twenty years, and the only reason Gus' and Sally's murders were not linked by the investigators was, frankly, sloppiness on our part. The detective who investigated Gus' murder just didn't give a damn. There were no forensics, no witnesses, so he let it go cold. If he had dug a little deeper, he would have discovered that Gus' girlfriend was murdered that same night, and that would have triggered a wider, deeper investigation. I don't think the Brotherhood would have risked that happening."

The inspector's face said she had a good point, and he turned that face on me. I scratched my head and shrugged. "I agree. It's a good point. But we know from Captain Jones that she had been 'disowned' by the Brotherhood, and that was synonymous with execution—and she died shortly after being visited by both Captain Jones and two members of the sect. In the face of that, I don't think the act they were both killed on the same night is enough. They were very far from home and probably in a hurry to get the job done and go back to Belfast."

She twisted her mouth into an ironic smile. "Well, that brings me to my second point. They were far from home—six hours by car—and this would be the only execution outside of Maine that they have carried out."

I frowned. "We don't know that."

"We kind of do. Chief McFarlane had spent years investigating these murders, and he gave us a comprehensive list. Every single one of them was killed in Maine."

The chief leaned forward with his elbows on the desk. "But you say that the Brotherhood sent people to see her . . ."

"Oh yes, they did, first Captain Jones and then, according to him, two other members. They came twice, and both times they left and she was still alive. One of the things that struck me as odd was that they had two opportunities to kill her—her brother had multiple opportunities to execute her—but they didn't. And frankly, the fact that the Jones family and the Rose family are so closely tied, in my view, is the reason they didn't kill her. Because she enjoyed Ewan Jones' protection. The point is, their MO consists of two basic elements: they operate in Maine, and they shoot their victims through the heart. But Sally was killed in New York, she was stabbed, and then she had her hands and feet removed. There is not a single other case of dismemberment among the cases attributed to the Brotherhood in the last twenty years."

The office fell very silent. The only sound was the drip, drip of water outside the chief's window and the desultory gusting of the wind. Finally, the chief sighed and glanced at me. "What are your comments, John?"

I shrugged. "I agree with everything Detective Dehan says. It is all unusual and uncharacteristic. But in the absence of an alternative theory that will explain these points, all we have is the Brotherhood. I have to add . . ." I smiled at Dehan, who was watching me without expression. "That I don't feel these oddities are impossible to explain. The fact that Sally was killed outside of Maine could signify that the Brotherhood is growing bold. It could also be explained by the fact that Sally was very important to them, being a member of a key family. The stabbing and the dismemberment are troubling, but she was stabbed in the heart, where the others were shot, and the removal of hands and feet may have a significance peculiar to her relationship with Captain Jones or Jeremiah Rose."

She shrugged. "That's a lot of maybes."

"It is also noteworthy, sir, that Gus' murder is totally consistent with their MO."

Dehan shook her head. "Not totally. He was killed outside Maine."

The chief drummed his fingers on the desk. "Carmen, have you an alternative theory?"

She made a noise that started out as a sigh and wound up as a low growl. "I'm working on it, sir."

"Care to share?"

"Um . . . Sir, right now it's like a collection of odd bits that I am trying to fit together. If you can give me just a little longer, I can tell you more."

He gave a single nod and turned to me. "Meantime, what do you want to do?"

"I think we need to hand this information over to the Feds."

He did more nodding. "I agree." He paused and then smiled. "Leave it with me. I'll call AD Skinner and send him what we have. Then I'll have a word with my contacts in the media and make it look like we are doing the bureau's work for them."

FIFTEEN

On the way down the stairs, Dehan punched me on the shoulder.

"The guy, the one who was hanging out with Sally and Gus, he was in the system, Leon Cohen."

I stopped dead and stared at her. "How the hell did you get that so fast?"

She continued a couple of steps, then turned and grinned at me. "That's not important right now—oh, and also, you know my methods, Watson, apply them. The important thing is that he is in the system, class A misdemeanor, possession of coke."

"An Ivy League misdemeanor. How did you find him so fast?"

"As I said, Stone, you know my methods . . ."

She turned and continued down the stairs. I followed, saying, "No, I don't. That is precisely what I am asking."

She nodded over her shoulder. "Quite so. So what I am thinking is, we should go and visit Leon and ask him about his friends, all those years back."

We had reached the entrance to the detectives' room. I stopped. "You have his address?"

She took my arm and steered me toward the exit. "Yup, and his phone number."

"How? You were ten minutes behind me!"

"You know, I know I said moussaka, but what haven't we had for a long time? Roast lamb. And this weather. This is perfect weather for roast lamb." She propelled me gently down the stairs toward the parking lot, saying, "You want to drive or shall I?"

I crossed the wet road, opened the driver's door, and frowned at her across the roof. "I'll drive, you talk."

I climbed in, and she got in beside me as I turned the key in the ignition and fired up the big growler. "There isn't a lot to say yet, Stone. Leon Cohen, I guess his parents were fans of Leonard, right? Rich family, big house on Long Island, eleven Sinclair Drive, King's Point. Bit of a playboy, likes to party hard, too hard sometimes, making his own fortune as a commodities broker . . ."

I smiled with my mouth and scowled with my eyes. The windshield wipers squeaked and thudded.

"Come on, Dehan! You were five minutes behind me. How the hell did you get all this information in five minutes? And why didn't you mention it to the chief?"

She edged around in her seat and regarded me with a small, one-sided smile. "You know what I am going to say. So let's focus on the case, big guy."

My answer was a grunt followed by a sigh as I pulled onto the expressway and headed for the Throgs Neck Bridge. She wagged a finger at me.

"You know that you are not satisfied with the Sacred Brotherhood explanation. It does not quite explain everything."

I shook my head. "I wouldn't say that, Dehan. We can't say that until we have all the evidence, and we can't get that without the Feds. Besides . . ." I shook my head again. "I don't know what you think this guy can tell you that Maya and Ben haven't told us already."

"Yeah," she said with a grin. "I know."

"Smart-ass. What do you think he can tell us?"

She didn't answer for a long while. She just sat smiling at me. It was unsettling. I glanced at her a couple of times, but she just kept smiling. Finally, as we sped out over the water and wet, blustery winds whipped across the bridge along the East River, dragging rain with them and hammering the car, making the steering wheel wobble, she sighed and said, "Really?"

"What?"

"Do you really want to know what I hope to get from Leon?"

"Yes, Dehan, of course I do. Stop playing silly games. What is this all about?"

"I hope to find out who killed Gus."

I stared at her. The car swerved, and I gripped the wheel. "Gus?"

"Mm-hm."

"You think Leon killed Gus? Based on what?"

"No, I just think he can help us find out who did." She looked out the windshield where the rain and the spray were obscuring the approaching Little Bay intersection. Suddenly, she became serious. "Something happened that night, Stone, and I don't buy that the Brotherhood suddenly, after all those years, decided to change their behavior, throw caution to the wind, and kill Gus and Sally in such bizarre ways. Something else happened, and it was that something else that has made this case so hard to crack for all these years. I'll go further . . ." She wagged her finger at me again. "This case is not about religion, moral deviance, or sex. This case is about something else."

I raised an eyebrow at her. "Yeah? What's it about?"

She raised her own eyebrow right back at me. "Power. It's about power."

"That's pretty general, can't you be more precise?"

"Not yet, nope."

We took the Cross Island Parkway, then came off onto Northern Boulevard and followed it around through tossing, wet trees under sagging skies to Great Neck Road and then West Shore Road, until we finally came to Kings Point. There, we turned onto Kings Point Road and then Sinclair Drive, where we pulled into a magnificent mansion among sodden lawns and dripping trees.

I killed the engine and looked at Dehan. "You know he's in?"

She nodded. "I called him."

I nodded back at her. "Okay, you made your point."

"What point, Stone?"

"It is a real pain in the ass to be excluded." I pointed at her. "You feel really smug right now, like I used to. But I get it is not fun being on this end. Can we stop now?"

She tossed her head from side to side. "Not quite yet, Dr. Watson. I think I might have a surprise for you, and nobody is going to deprive me of that."

I rolled my eyes and climbed out into the heavy drizzle. She got out too, and we pulled up our collars against the cold wind as we made our way to the front porch. Dehan rang the bell, and we stood and stamped our feet for a minute until a cute young woman in a French maid's uniform opened the door for us.

Dehan showed her badge and said, "Detective Carmen Dehan. I made an appointment over the telephone with Mr. Cohen."

"Sure. He's in the drawing room. He's expecting you."

The place was old world and mahogany, with hardwood floors strewn with real Persian rugs. She led us past a couple of statues of Venus and a couple of Greek philosophers and into a drawing room, which was about the size of my house. The walls were paneled in oak, the bookcases were protected by leaded glass, and there were Chesterfields arranged around the open fire. Leon was standing, looking out the French windows at the rain saturating an acre of lawn, and turned as we came in. He hadn't changed much since the photograph in the Waddling Duck, but he was less a boy now and more a man, he was better groomed, and his clothes were chosen to command respect, rather than blend into the crowd.

"Detective Dehan and . . . ?"

I showed him my badge. "John Stone."

He gestured toward the fire and the Chesterfields. "Please, can I offer you a drink? Some coffee?"

Dehan answered, "Coffee would be nice." She smiled at him like he was somebody she'd like to be friends with. "It's a hell of a day."

"It sure is. Alice? Coffee, please, and some cake."

This last was directed at the maid, who bobbed and withdrew.

There was no coffee table to bang your shins on. The Chesterfields were ranged around a large rug before a fireplace that was six feet tall and almost five across. Within it, logs burned and spat sparks onto the hearth. Lamp tables and occasional tables were arranged strategically so that you could put your coffee, or your gin and tonic, beside you. It was very civilized.

I sat opposite Leon in an armchair, and Dehan sat next to him at the far end of the sofa, with her legs crossed toward him. I might not have been there. I knew she was playing him, but that didn't make me like it any better. Leon addressed her.

"I wasn't very clear on the phone, Detective, what it was exactly you wanted to discuss with me?"

"Well . . ." She glanced at me and actually looked bashful. "We run a cold-case unit at the Forty-Third Precinct, in the Bronx . . ."

Leon gave a laugh that was urbane. "Oh, my! That is very brave of you."

I felt like telling him I ran the damn thing, but I let them get on with it. Dehan was saying, "Well, it's not as dangerous as it seems. Mainly routine paperwork and the occasional interview, and to be perfectly honest, most cases stay cold . . ."

She paused, watching him, smiling. Something curious happened to his face. I couldn't pinpoint it, but I felt a quickening of excitement in my gut. Dehan shrugged and made it look demure.

"Thing is, we are reviewing a case that is nearly ten years old now, and in my honest opinion, it doesn't stand a chance in hell of being cleared up." She leaned forward and laughed. He laughed with her. "But we have to go through the motions, right? And I happened to notice that in previous investigations, the detectives overlooked the fact that you were a witness."

He did a good job of looking amazed, but it was fake. Dehan saw it, and I realized she'd set it up. He laughed. "I? I was not a witness to any crime ten years ago! At least, not that I recall."

"I know!" She laughed and laid a hand on his forearm. "I know. Sorry! I should not have sprung it like that. But you were a friend of Sally Jones and Gus McBride, right?"

His mouth opened and closed several times. "Um . . . names . . ." He shook his head.

She pulled one of the photographs from her pocket and showed it to him. "How about pictures?"

"Oh! Sally! And of course, Gus. His name was Gus, of course!"

"Right?"

"Yes, of course, forgive me."

"You guys were pretty tight back then."

He shrugged, made the kind of face that said it wasn't so much. "Well, tight, I wouldn't go so . . ."

She pulled out the other pictures and showed them to him. "Right? I mean . . ." She laughed and gestured around her at the house. "I mean, socially they were not in your class. I guess you didn't invite them to tea on Sunday, to meet the folks! But when you were out being a bad boy . . ." She paused to wipe her finger under her nose and sniff loudly, he blanched, and she laughed. "I read your file. Don't worry about it. But what I am saying is, when you were out on the town, prowling the bars, these guys were your go-to crowd, right?"

"Um . . ."

"There it is, right there." She pointed at the pictures. "Right there."

He nodded. "I guess, for a few months, we were close acquaintances. But not more than that."

She grew serious. "Sure. Sure. Listen, Leon, may I call you Leon?"

"Of course."

"I have zero interest in your recreational habits. Zero. But I want to find the SOB who killed Sally. You get that, right?"

"Of course."

"So I am figuring, Sally was a bit wild, am I right?"

He laughed nervously and nodded. "Yes, she was a little wild."

"She walked a fine line, right?"

"She did that . . . Look, Detective Dehan, I was very young back then and did some foolish things. I really don't need this stuff surfacing again. It could do severe damage to my career . . ."

"Leon." She reached out and squeezed his wrist again. "Believe me, I don't want any of this stuff to come back and bite you in the ass. That is the last thing that I want. You level with me, and I promise you I will keep you out of it. You have my word."

"I am very grateful. Naturally, I will level with you in every way I can."

There was a knock at the door, and Dehan flopped back in her chair. The door opened, and the French maid brought in a silver tray with a pot of coffee, three china cups, and a small cake stand. We went through the ceremony of distributing cups and cakes, and the maid left again.

Dehan stuffed her face with cake and spoke with her mouth full, wiping cream from her lips with her thumb.

"See, I have always believed that Sally was trading coke and girls. Was that true?"

"Um . . ."

"I mean, did you buy your coke from her?"

He closed his eyes, took a deep breath, and said, "On a couple of occasions, I, we, the crowd, bought a gram from her. It wasn't a regular thing . . ."

"I am not interested in that. What I am interested in is that she had it available."

"Yes, she did."

"And how about girls?"

"I think, how can I put this? I think she facilitated contact between girls and men who were looking for some fun."

"Right. That's a dangerous line of work."

"I wouldn't know, but I would imagine."

She drained her cup and sighed loudly. "So I am figuring that Gus was her muscle. First Ben, right? Then he moved on and Gus took over."

He hesitated, but he couldn't risk being caught in a lie, so he nodded. "Yes, I got the impression that was the setup."

She nodded for a bit, then frowned and shook her head. "But that's what confuses me. If what she was after was muscle, Ben was her guy. I mean, he's one of the best MMA fighters in the country. Gus was tough, but he was not in the same class as Ben."

He spread his hands. "I can't answer that. It's true that it doesn't make sense . . ."

She stared at him, waiting.

Finally, to fill the void, he said, "Perhaps he offered her something else."

"Like what?"

"I don't know."

"But you were there. They were close. What was their relationship based on?"

He had become nervous. He hid it well, but he was nervous. "I honestly didn't know them that well, Detective. We were drinking buddies. That was it."

"Sure! Sure, I get that." She stared at him a moment with no expression, then burst out, "You're a pretty weird friend for them, aren't you?"

"Well, um, I don't know . . ."

"I mean, her type were tough, hard guys. You, with all due respect, are a smart, Ivy League college kid. What did you bring to the group?"

He smiled and sagged back in his chair. "Fine, Detective, the truth is that I was looking for some raw excitement at that time. Sally was looking for what Sally was always looking for, money. I had money, and lots of it—more than she could ever dream of having—so she welcomed me to the group. If Sally welcomed you, you were in. It lasted a couple of months, and I moved on."

"Did you move on before she was murdered?"

He looked down at his cup, puffed out his cheeks, and blew. "I was there one night, midweek, we had a typically wild night. I went home. When I next went back, I learned that they had been murdered. That was the end of it."

We were silent for a moment. The rain lashed silently against the triple-glazed French doors, and the trees bowed and tossed silently under the downpour.

Dehan said suddenly, "What was wild about it?"

"I'm sorry?"

"You said it was a wild night. What was wild about it?"

"It was just a typical night. Lots of drinking, girls . . ."

Her face was hard, expressionless; her eyes were penetrating. "Anything special happen? Anything unusual or out of the ordinary?"

He shook his head. "No, nothing special. She was a big flirt. I always assumed she upset somebody and they punished her."

She smiled. "I guess that was it." She put her hands on her knees and stood. He and I followed suit. "Thanks for your time and your hospitality, Leon. I'm sorry if I was a bit hard on you. Comes with the territory."

Her gaze drifted to the French doors, and she walked over to look out at the sodden lawns, the great trees turning shades of ochre, red, and orange, half concealing the outhouses that fringed the lawn.

"This sure is a beautiful house. I always dreamed of living in a house like this." She gave him a meaningful smile. "Detective's salary don't quite cover the mortgage, though." She nodded across the lawn. "You have horses?"

"No, no. I never had much interest in horses, I'm afraid. Those are no longer stables."

She winked. "Horsepower, not horses, right?"

He laughed. "Quite!"

Now she jerked her head at me. "Stone here, he has an ancient Jaguar, 1964. Brought it over from England with the original plates. It takes seven seconds . . ." She turned to me. "Or is it seven hours? To get from naught to sixty!"

He looked at me with interest. "A '64 Jaguar, right-hand drive?"

"Yeah, a Mark II."

"That's a nice car."

I managed to sound bored and asked him, "You're interested in cars?"

He shrugged. "I'm a privileged dilettante. It's not quite a hobby, I am no expert, but I am interested." He smiled at Dehan and gestured toward the buildings across the lawn. "I have a small collection of classic cars. In fact, one of your colleagues was here just the other day. One of my cars was stolen."

I winced like I cared. "That must hurt."

He nodded. "Yeah, this particular one hurt. It was the jewel in the crown, so to speak. A '65 Mustang Fastback. Pristine, once owned by Steve McQueen."

I whistled, and Dehan said, "Whoa!"

I asked him, "What's that worth?"

"It's insured for a million, but it's probably worth more than that."

I made a "tsk!" sound of sympathy, then frowned. "How did that fall under the jurisdiction of the Forty-Third?"

"Ah." He gave a small laugh. "It was actually stolen from a lockup in the Bronx." My frown demanded more, so he went on, "Sometimes I like to drive them. What's the point of having them if you don't drive them, right?"

"Right."

"So if I take them into town and have a few drinks, I leave them in the lockup."

"In the Bronx . . ."

He laughed. "At Manhattan prices? You bet!"

I nodded and moved toward the door. "Well, thanks for your time, Mr. Cohen. I hope they find your car."

He followed us, his urbane manner now fully restored. "Anytime, I am only sorry I could not be more helpful."

He stood watching from the porch as we crossed the wet gravel to the Jag, but he wasn't watching us, he was watching the car.

SIXTEEN

WE SLIPPED THROUGH AVENUES OF DENSE AUTUMN trees, some still green, others in various degrees of brown, russet, and orange, the headlamps making broken, oily light on the road ahead. Dehan was ensconced in the angle between the seat and the door, her left arm clenched under her armpit, her right hand tapping her teeth with her fingernail as she stared unseeing at the passing trees.

I was mad, so I kept silent, wondering if I was mad at her for not sharing her thoughts, or at myself for not having seen what she had seen. After a moment, she glanced at me.

"This was del Rio's guy."

"I got that."

"You mad?"

"I'm trying not to be. How did you know?"

She sighed, spread her hands, and let them flop in her lap. "I told you to look at the photograph of Sally and Gus sitting on the Mustang. The registration plate . . ."

"You didn't know what the missing Mustang's plate was. How could you know that?"

"I didn't, Stone. But the plate on the car Sally and Gus were on—the one you said you couldn't see—it had an 'M' and a 'Q' at the beginning, and it ended in 'N.' You said I was reaching, but how many words can you think of, between five and seven letters, that start 'MQ' and end in 'N'?"

I shook my head, narrowing my eyes at her. "That is an insane coincidence. The chances of that being the same car are immeasurably small."

"Yeah, but I don't think it is a coincidence."

I shook my head again and sighed. "You're losing me."

Before she could answer, the phone rang. It was Bernie from the bureau.

"Stone, for once, it's me calling you. I've been looking at the material you sent over. You want to talk me through it?"

"Yeah, sure. We're at Kings Point right now. Give me forty-five minutes and we'll meet you at your office."

"You got it." I hung up and, after a moment, asked Dehan, "So what is your theory? Even if this is the same Mustang, how does it tie in to Sally's and Gus' death? I am having trouble following your thinking."

She was staring out the side window at the passing hedgerows, so I was speaking to the back of her head. After a moment, she took a hold of her long hair and tied it into a knot. She still didn't look at me.

"Everything hinges," she said, "on who stole the Mustang." I drew breath, but she cut me short. "Don't ask me any more than that, Stone, because that's all I can tell you. Everything hinges on who stole the Mustang. The Mustang is central to this whole case."

We didn't talk a lot after that. We made our way across Queens and the Brooklyn Bridge, and then crawled our way to the Federal Plaza building. By the time we walked into Bernie's office, it was past lunchtime, and his desk was littered with sandwich bags and Tupperware, which he cleared away while wiping his mouth with a handkerchief.

"Sit, sit, sit!"

We sat in functional chairs, and behind him, and his littered desk, we were treated to a view of mist and rain over Duane Street. He sat and pulled over a file, leafed through it, refreshing his memory, and looked up and smiled.

"This is for real?"

I sighed a little ill-humoredly. "Of course it's for real, Bernie. You heard Chief McFarlane's testimony. The next day, he was executed in his own office."

He shrugged and shook his head. "You read about this stuff in novels, you see it on TV, but . . ."

"It's for real."

"So we have a team working on warrants right now. We want to search the temple, we want to search Jeremiah Rose's house and the houses of the Council, we also want access to bank accounts and documents. So that is going to take a little time, but we hope to have it sorted by tonight. Then we are going to raid them all simultaneously."

"You confident you'll get the warrants?"

"Yeah, I spoke to Judge Suzuki about an hour ago. All he is asking is we draft it right. The okay is as good as granted. You want in?"

He glanced from me to Dehan and back. She answered before me. "Yeah, I want to see Rose's papers with my own eyes. I figure they're in the church."

I nodded. "I agree. That place is a fortress. If they don't want you in there, they will make it hard. They might even use force."

"You're serious?"

"You better believe it, Bernie. They consider themselves Jesus' warriors, and they will use force. They made that very clear to us. Hell, how brazen do you need to be to walk into a police station, midmorning, and shoot the chief of police? And that's another thing, do not rely on the local PD to back you up. Half of them are members of the Brotherhood. I am serious. This is like Waco on steroids."

He held up both hands. "Okay, okay, I believe you. Now, explain something to me, because I am getting mixed messages, not least from your boss, Inspector Newman. Are we saying that Sally Jones is on the list of victims, or not? And what about Angus McBride?"

I drew breath, but Dehan spoke first. "We're not clear on that, Bernie. There is another line of inquiry, which, if it is correct, would mean that their murders—or at least Sally's—were not a federal matter. I think we'll know a lot more if we can get our hands on the Brotherhood's records."

Bernie spread his hands wide, hunched his shoulders, and nodded extravagantly. "Assuming that they keep records. They seem to me to be very careful people."

I cut in, "But they are also very methodical. My money is on records which are kept under lock and key, probably in the vaults under the church."

"A tad obvious."

"You want some advice?"

"From you? Always."

"Five minutes before the raid, we should take the mayor and Captain Jones into custody, for their own protection. I think they'll break easy and give us just about everything we need to know."

"What makes you think they'll break?"

Dehan answered, "Jones is wracked with guilt over his sister, and doubts about the Brotherhood. He gave us information that could get him killed if the Brotherhood found out. The mayor . . ."

She made a face and looked at me.

"Because he has a lot to lose. The original purpose of the Sacred Brotherhood of Christ might have been to execute servants of Satan, and I am pretty sure that is still what drives Jeremiah Rose, but I am equally sure that most of the members today are more interested in the privilege the Brotherhood provides, and the access to positions of power and wealth. I'm pretty sure the mayor is one of those, and if he is facing prosecution for murder, and a life sentence, he'll sing like a damned canary."

Dehan nodded. "Yeah, I'd say that's right."

We talked a little more, nailed down some details, and agreed to meet again at his office at six p.m. to take a chopper to Belfast.

"We'll get there about ten, have a briefing, and then start making our moves. We'll carry out the raids in the small hours. Based on what you've given us here, the AD basically wants to shut down Belfast for the duration of the raid."

I nodded. "He's got it about right."

"You and Carmen will be with me. We'll take the church, and there will be a SWAT team from Augusta who will take control of the station house. We also have the National Guard on alert." He laughed out loud. "Boy! You better be right about this!"

We left shortly after and rode the elevator down to the lobby in silence. By the time we stepped outside, the rain had eased to a slight drizzle, but there was a cold wind that fingered its way through your clothes and made your skin crawl and shudder.

As we made our way to the car, Dehan pulled out her cell and stood by the passenger door, dialing. I waited, watching her. She met my eye and said, "I want to talk to Maya again."

"Now?"

"We have time. I just need . . . Hi, Maya, it's Detective Carmen Dehan . . . Yeah, not bad. Listen, I need to go over a few things with you . . . It's pretty urgent. Where are you . . . ? Okay, can you spare us fifteen minutes? We'll be there in . . ." She glanced at me. "Half an hour?"

I made an "I have no idea I don't know where she is" face and shrugged.

She ignored me and said, "Cool. We'll be there ASAP."

She hung up and opened the passenger door. "She's on her way home. We're going to meet her there."

She climbed in and slammed the door. I got in after her and turned the key in the ignition. "Where is home?"

"1170 Thieriot."

I headed south on Spruce Street, toward the FDR, and after a moment asked, "Are you going to tell me what it is you hope to get from Maya that we didn't get before?"

"Sure." She thought for a while, staring out at the river and the heavy clouds that still hung heavily over the city. "I want to know . . ." she said cautiously, like she was lining up the words to get them in the right order, "what went down between Sally, Gus, and Leon. I want to know how, and why, the Mustang made the transition from Gus to Leon, and I want to know who has it now." She turned finally and gave me a very direct stare. "Because whoever has it now, killed . . ." She trailed off, staring past me at the roof of the car, then finished, "killed Sally."

I shook my head and drove in silence for a while, then shook it again. "I don't know how you can possibly know that, Dehan." I looked at her. "Where is the evidence? What are you basing that on?"

She shrugged, then grinned. "It's logic, Captain."

I raised an eyebrow. "But not as we know it."

She shrugged again. "Think it through."

We beat the rush hour to the Bronx and made it to Maya's apartment in just over half an hour. The apartment was in a large Victorian redbrick with sash windows and an elaborate scroll over the door. We rang the bell, and after a couple of minutes, Maya let us in and led us up a flight of carpeted stairs to a top floor that had been converted from bedrooms into a snug apartment. She showed us into a living room at the front of the house, overlooking Thieriot and Gleason, and sat us around a glass coffee table, on white imitation leather chairs. She took the sofa.

"I'm really not sure what more I can tell you, Detective Dehan. It was a long time ago, and I told you everything I remember the other day."

Dehan smiled. It was a nice, engaging smile. "I know. There are just a few details I'd like to get clear. You know how it is, sometimes the tiniest detail can make all the difference."

Maya glanced at me. "I guess." She looked back at Dehan. "What do you want to know?"

She sank back in her chair, and her gaze was lost out the window. When she spoke, her voice was distant, like she was seeing something other than the bellying clouds over the rooftops.

"I need to know what went on between those three on the last few nights, the week before she died. Something changed in that week. Something changed in the stuff they talked about. Something changed . . ." She turned her gaze on Maya and wagged a finger at her. "Something changed between Gus and the nerdy guy."

Maya frowned, and Dehan pulled the pictures from her jacket and handed them to her. "Remember him?"

Maya took them and gave a little gasp. "Oh my god! Look at Sally! And Gus . . . and . . . what was his name . . . ?"

"Leon."

Maya looked up and snapped her fingers. "Leon! That was it! Leon, he was funny, but Sally used to play him a lot. He had money. I think he came from a rich banking family or something. They used him. It wasn't right, really, but I guess he got something out of it or he wouldn't keep coming back, right?"

Dehan nodded. "So that last week . . ."

Maya stared at the photographs and wrinkled her brow. "Did something change? Yeah, I guess it did. It got kind of intense. Funny how seeing the pictures can bring it back like that. But it was Gus and Sally, not Gus and Leon. That last week, they had a thing going, and it got kind of serious. Leon was sweet on Sally, and she used to play him along, and also play him and Gus off each other. Leon had been pestering Gus about something."

Dehan leaned forward. "Pestering him how?"

"He wanted something from him, I can't remember what. To be honest, I'm not sure I ever even knew. I used to let them get on with it, you know? They were a bit cliquey sometimes. So I do remember that Gus got kind of mad with Leon in the end and told him to leave him alone. He was always giving Sally stuff, jewelry, clothes, money . . . like he was buying her."

"And Leon tried to compete?"

She thought about it and screwed up her face. "Not exactly. He could have bought and sold Gus a hundred times over. No, it was more like he wanted Sally to like him for who he was. And that Sunday, before she died, the bar was pretty quiet, and I remember there was suddenly a big ruckus at the bar. Sally was laughing out loud and so was Gus, and Leon looked real upset."

Dehan reached over and took hold of Maya's hands in hers. "Maya, it may be nothing, or it could be real important, but I need you to try really hard and think what that ruckus was about. Try to remember, any tiny detail could be key."

Maya sighed deeply and bit her lip. "You hear so much about false memories, and I might say something that is not important at all, but you might think . . ." She trailed off.

Dehan shook her head. "Believe me, between us, we have over forty years of experience, and we know how to distinguish what's important from what isn't. If there is anything, however trivial . . ."

Maya looked like she might suddenly burst into tears. "Well, there is one thing, but it seems so stupid. I don't even know why it stuck in my mind. If you hadn't asked . . ."

"What is it?"

She shrugged. "A napkin. When they were laughing, Leon got up and marched away from the bar. He said something, it sounded like a number, but Gus just seemed to wave this paper napkin at him. Then he folded it and put it in his wallet." She shrugged again. "Leon seemed to calm down and returned to the bar. That was it. I am sure it's not important. I wouldn't want Gus to get into trouble . . ."

We both stared at her. She blinked, reading something in our expressions, but not knowing quite what.

Dehan said, "Maya, Gus is dead. You didn't know?"

She put her fingers to her mouth. "Oh, my god . . . ! How . . . ?"

"He was murdered the same night as Sally."

"Oh, but that's . . . I had no idea."

"You didn't read it in the papers?"

She shook her head. "I guess they were focused on Sally. I noticed Gus had stopped showing up, but he was that kind of guy. I thought maybe, you know, he was on the run . . ."

SEVENTEEN

The cold wind had broken up the clouds some, and though the moon was not visible, its light touched the edges of the clouds, where the sky showed through the open gaps. We were sitting with Bernie in an unmarked Dodge, watching the Church of the Sacred Brotherhood of Christ. It was still and silent, like Belfast. Nothing moved save the leaves in the small, cold breeze, and the clouds as they twisted slowly across the moonlight.

Fifty feet away, on the far side of the main entrance, there was a van. On its side panel, it said something about construction and maintenance. It too was still and silent, though we knew there was a SWAT team waiting inside it.

After a moment, we heard a crackle in our earpieces, and a voice spoke.

"All units in position. Awaiting confirmation from teams A and B . . ." We waited a few seconds longer and the crackle came again. "Confirmed, teams A and B have their targets in custody. You are clear to go. Repeat, teams A and B have their targets in custody. You are clear to go."

Bernie snapped, "Okay, all teams go! Repeat, all teams go!"

As he said it, we were climbing out of the car. The rear of the van burst open, and a stream of men in helmets and flak jackets streamed toward the main entrance of the church. Meanwhile, I knew the rear access was covered too, by men in the parking lot by the self storage units, and in the undergrowth in the alleys. If there was anyone in the church, that was where they were going to stay.

We moved in at a steady run. Ahead of us, two guys with a battering ram smashed the lock and kicked in the door, then charged in. We followed, letting the assault team go ahead. Their voices echoed under the high ceilings: "FBI! FBI! Come out with your hands in the air! Make yourself known! FBI!" And the shouts were marked in counterpoint by the cry of, "Clear! Clear!" as room after room was found empty.

Then, two men in helmets and body armor burst through the doors Dehan and I had so recently crossed to go and see Jeremiah. Their assault rifles were at their shoulders as they scanned the hall, the stairs, and the gallery landing. The whole thing took less than a second, and suddenly there was a dull, dry clatter from the gallery, splinters of wood erupted from the doors, and plaster exploded from the walls. The two men staggered back. One of them fell on his back, groaning. I ran forward with Dehan and dragged the fallen guy back. The doors swung closed, shuddering under the continued fire.

Bernie was shouting, "Man down! Man down! We need a medical team!" and as he said it, the second guy sank to his knees, holding his leg. There was a lot of blood. The SWAT team leader was shouting something about falling back, but I was watching Dehan.

She wasn't listening to him; she was staring at the door and asking me, "Did you see him?"

I nodded. "He was directly opposite, lying on his belly."

The team was falling back. Bernie was shouting at us to follow. I saw Dehan reach down and pick up the fallen guy's rifle and throw it to me. I caught it and frowned. Then she kicked open the door again and was firing up at the gallery as she did so, screaming at me, "Cover me! Cover me!"

I had no choice. I opened fire, spraying the landing with hot lead. From the corner of my eye, I saw her jump and roll. She came up on one knee directly under the shooter and emptied the magazine into the underside of the gallery. He lay perfectly still in the ringing silence.

I ran up the stairs with Dehan just behind me, and we covered the doors to the chapel. The young man called David lay dead on the floor in a spreading pool of blood. Dehan leaned over the banister and shouted, "Clear!"

Bernie and the depleted SWAT team came streaming up the stairs and positioned themselves with their weapons trained on the door. Bernie's face was flushed. He scowled at Dehan. "Don't ever..."

I cut him short. "That's a chapel in there. Beyond it, where the apse should be, there is a room, high, domed ceiling, round table, bookcases, et cetera. I get the impression it's the Council Chamber. My money is on the faithful being in there."

He stared at me for a long moment. "No more stunts like that, Stone."

I looked at Dehan. "No more stunts, Dehan. You heard the man."

She shrugged. "We're here, aren't we?"

I turned back to Bernie. "They knew we were coming. How?"

"Are you kidding me, Stone? An organization like this, with Augusta PD involved?"

Dehan cut in, "Listen, we can't just stand here and talk. We lose momentum and this becomes a Waco standoff. We have to storm the Council Chamber now."

The head of the SWAT team shook his head. "Detective, with all due respect, that's how lives are lost. We already have two men down..."

"And you're going to have a damn sight more if we don't close this thing down." She turned and took the assault rifle from me. "Coming?"

I started to say, "Dehan, wait!"

But she had turned to the guys and shouted, "Stand back!" and next thing, she had yanked the door to the chapel open and hurled herself in, rolling across the floor to the cover of a large statue of Jesus mounted upon a horse, with a sword in his hand.

Nothing happened. She covered the nave with her weapon. I slipped in and moved across the back of the chapel, checking among the pews and behind the pillars. When I came to the far aisle, I shouted, "Clear so far!" and we started to move down toward the altar.

The team came in, followed by Bernie. Dehan came out from behind the statue and trotted toward the apse. I moved quickly to the altar, checked it, and shouted, "Clear!"

Then the door to the apse opened and all hell broke loose.

I saw Dehan hit the floor as four men came out and opened up with automatic rifles. Two of the SWAT guys went down in a shower of plaster, gilt, and wood splinters from the pews. I heard screams of pain and Bernie's voice shouting for backup.

Then the team was retreating through the doors, dragging their casualties with them. The hail of lead stopped, and a young voice shouted, "Return to the abyss of hell! Enter the House of the Lord at your peril!"

That was followed by Dehan's voice shouting, "Freeze! You're under arrest! Drop your weapons!"

I felt a surge of panic and leapt from behind the altar, training my weapon on them and adding my voice to Dehan's. "Drop your weapons! You are under arrest! Put your hands where I can see them!"

That was never going to happen. I saw the guy nearest her shift his weapon toward her. I squeezed the trigger, his body seemed to whiplash, and I saw a plume of blood and gore erupt from his back, where the slug exited. Almost simultaneously, I saw Dehan's weapon kick, and he doubled up and went down. If we had picked separate targets, we might have stood a chance, but we wasted both shots on the same guy.

Of the remaining three, one stepped forward and slammed the stock of his rifle into her head. I bellowed and ran forward, not seeing the other guy, who had lined me up and pulled the trigger. He was shooting at a moving target and that saved my life, but it didn't save me from the searing pain that tore through my chest. I fired back, but the pain was excruciating and my shots went wide. They dragged Dehan into the chamber by her heels and slammed the door as the room rocked and I fell flat on my face on the stone floor.

I don't know how long I lay there, but at some point, I became aware that I was staring at a flagstone. There was an agonizing throbbing in my shoulder and a sticky pool of blood beside my head. There was also total silence.

I lifted my face and looked over at the door to the apse. It was open, and there were three boys there, probably in their twenties, kneeling and holding rifles. Their dead comrade lay just in front of them.

They were watching me, and the middle one said, "I don't think he's dead." Then he raised his voice. "Are you dead?"

It was a bizarre, surreal moment, and it made me laugh in spite of the pain. "Yes," I said. "I'm dead. You shot me, didn't you?"

I rolled painfully on my side and explored the wound with my fingers. I had been luckier than any man deserves. It had torn through my pectoral at an angle and missed the chest cavity, but it still hurt like hell.

"Can you walk?"

I scowled at him. "You shot me in the chest, not my legs, you dumb asshole." I struggled to my knees. "Why don't you finish me off?"

"Because you're going to take a message from the Elder Brother to the forces of Satan."

At that moment, I looked past them and saw Dehan. She was

on the table, kneeling, gagged, and with her hands and feet bound, exhibited for me to see. I felt the hot rage start in my belly and got to my feet.

"Hurt her and I swear..."

"Be careful, cop." It was Jeremiah. He stood behind his boys, leaning one hand on the doorframe. "Don't go saying anything you might later regret."

With that, he turned and went back to the table, where he grabbed Dehan's hair and yanked fiercely so that she cried out and fell on her side. From there, he dragged her savagely off the table so that she fell to the stone floor.

I cried out and ran forward, shouting for him to stop, but ran into three rifle barrels rammed in my face. Beyond them, Jeremiah Rose was snarling at me. "Don't hurt her or you swear what, cop? What will you do if I hurt her?"

I held up my right hand. "Stop! I'll do anything, just leave her be. Don't hurt her, please!"

He turned away, bent down, and dragged her to her feet, then shoved her forward, Dehan hobbling where her ankles had been bound. The three boys parted, and I saw inside that there were four more, following Jeremiah. Seven total. I stared into Dehan's eyes as she hobbled past, and I saw real fear.

The kids with guns fanned out and took up positions around the altar, training their guns on the entrance to the chapel at the far end. I watched, with my heart pounding and my head rocking, as Jeremiah led Dehan up the steps to the altar.

"What are you doing? Are you insane?"

He pointed at me, and his eyes were crazed with rage. "I told you, boy! You want to be careful with that mouth of yours!" To the two nearest boys, he said, "Get her up!"

And they grabbed her by her shoulders and her legs and lifted her body onto the altar.

"What do you think, boy? This Jewess a fitting sacrifice for our Lord? To make you motherfucking Satan worshippers get out of my church?" Suddenly, he was roaring, "You think she is a fitting whore to sacrifice to our Lord Jesus the Avenger?"

I lifted my right hand again, my left dangling uselessly by my side. "Please, Brother Jeremiah, I will do anything you want, anything you ask, just please, I beg of you, don't hurt her. What do you want from us?"

He pointed toward the doors of the chapel. "I want you to go out there and tell them Satan-loving deviants that my demands must be met. What are my demands? I shall tell you what my demands are! I want five million dollars in a suitcase! I want a plane to take us to Mexico, and I want you and your wife to come along for the ride."

He laughed at the astonishment on my face.

"Of course I know, you dumb asshole! The whole of America knows! You're celebrities now. The infallible duo! The Cold Case Masters with the unbroken record. Detectives Stone and Dehan, America's sweethearts. There is no way they are going to allow anything to happen to you. Why, I bet NBC or CBS will even put up the money for the ransom. Why, I think I should ask for double—ten million bucks! What do you say, boy?"

I hesitated a moment, and his eyes seemed to penetrate right to my soul.

"What are you wondering? What will I do if you, or they, refuse to cooperate?" He pulled a large hunting knife from his belt behind his back. "I will cut off her hands and her feet, one by one, just like Sally, and offer them to you as mementos of your idyllic marriage. How does that sound, boy?"

My head reeled, and the room rocked. "So it was you. Why, why the dismemberment? Why did you do it?"

He strode toward me and thrust his face into mine. His pale eyes were mad, the pupils small, black pinpricks. His skin flushed red, and he screamed, "I can do anything I like, motherfucker! I can do anything I like because I am the Elect of the Lord! So fuck you!"

I backed away a step, and he pointed at the doors to the chapel.

"Go! Go and tell them that I am their Lord and they must obey! Tell them my demands! Ten million bucks in two suitcases and a plane to take us to Mexico! And you, miserable, sniveling wretch, and your Jew-whore wife, to serve as my hostages! Go! Tell your Satan-loving master my demands!"

I looked past him at Dehan's terrified face, twisted toward me on the stone altar. Then I turned and hurried toward the door. I pulled it open and found the landing empty. Even the body of the boy Dehan had shot was gone. I peered over the railings down toward the area below. There was no one.

"Bernie! Bernie!"

There was no reply. No sound in the building. I staggered down the stairs and pushed my way out into the reception area. Red-and-blue lights flashed through the glass door, pulsing against the white walls. I struggled across to the door and pulled it open.

A moment later, I was blinded by spotlights, and a voice roared at me, "Raise your hands! Raise both your hands or I'll shoot!"

"I can't," I said, but my voice was too weak to carry. "I can't. I'm shot..."

EIGHTEEN

"It's John Stone!"

The shout went up and was taken up by more voices: "It's Detective Stone!"

"It's Stone!"

And then there were other voices, their speakers invisible behind the glaring spots. "Where is Detective Dehan?"

"Detective Stone! Where is your wife?"

"Have you abandoned her inside?"

"What have they done with her? Is she dead?"

And then there were strong arms and hands grabbing me, dragging me away, out of the glare, toward an ambulance that was standing there, its lights pulsing with the police cars on the wet asphalt, the sodden trees, and the walls of the houses. Bernie was there, looking worried and mad, and with him was a big man in a suit.

Bernie was saying, "What the hell were you thinking?"

I heard my own voice mumble, like somebody else was speaking. "I couldn't let her go alone . . ."

"Are you insane?"

"Stand back, please!" There were a couple of paramedics peeling off my jacket and cutting my shirt.

I glanced at them. "It's through and through."

Bernie was shaking his head. "Jesus!"

The big guy said, "I'm Assistant Director Skinner, I need to know what's going down in there. Are you up to it?"

I nodded. "They have her hostage. There are seven young men with assault rifles, plus Jeremiah Rose. They will do anything for him. They are fanatical. They have moved into the chapel and have Detective Dehan bound and gagged on the altar. He has demands..."

I winced as the paramedic gave me a shot and started dressing the wound.

Skinner said, "What kind of demands?"

"What you'd expect. Ten million bucks in a couple of suitcases and a flight to Mexico. Dehan and I go along as hostages. He reckons he can play on the media."

His voice was deep, his eyes searching. "And if we don't play ball?"

"He'll cut off her hands and her feet, one by one, until we do."

He sighed and turned to Bernie. "We need a skilled negotiator. Call Neville. I want him here within the hour."

I shook my head. "No. You can't do that. You send a negotiator in there, he will kill the negotiator and then he'll cut off one of her hands or feet."

"You can't possibly know that, Stone. We have a lot of experience dealing with this kind of situation..."

I growled at him, "This kind of situation? What kind of situation? When have you ever seen a situation like this? A three-hundred-year-old cult that controls a small city and spends twenty years systematically assassinating people who stray from the fold? Then kidnaps a police detective and demands ten million dollars and a plane to Mexico? That kind of situation? You have a lot of experience with that kind of situation?"

"Calm down, Detective Stone."

"Don't fucking tell me to calm down, Skinner. That's my wife in there . . ."

"I am aware of that, and that is precisely why we need to put this in the hands of an expert."

"Bullshit! And let's get this clear, if anything happens to her because you didn't listen to me, I am coming after you." I stabbed his chest with my finger. "So no damned expert negotiators go in there. I go in there, and I tell him that his demands will be met. Unconditionally!"

He shook his head. "You can't do that. You have neither the authority nor the jurisdiction."

"Really? Watch me."

I reached inside Bernie's coat, pulled out his Glock, and shoved it down the front of my pants, into my crotch. I then pulled out my shirt so it covered the top of my pants, shrugged my jacket back on, and heard the annoyed voice of the paramedic behind me.

"Hey! I'm not done!"

Then I was pushing through the crowd toward the TV van that was parked on the other side of the road, filming the scene. There was a female anchor there who saw me coming and hurried over.

"Detective Stone! Can you tell us what is going on? What is happening in there?"

I could hear Skinner and Bernie running up behind me. I pointed back at the church. "My wife is captive in there, and Jeremiah Rose is threatening to sacrifice her, on the altar of Christ the Avenger, if he is not paid ten million dollars and given a plane to Mexico, where he plans to take me and my wife as hostages. I have discussed the matter with AD Skinner, of the Federal Bureau of Investigation, and he agrees with me that the best thing is for me to return inside and tell Jeremiah Rose that we will meet his demands. We cannot, under any circumstances, afford to lose an officer of the caliber of Detective Dehan."

Skinner and Bernie were staring at me like they wanted to eat my heart with French fries.

The anchor asked, "But where will this money come from? That is a huge sum..."

"A donor has come forward. That is all I can say at this stage."

"So soon? I mean, you've just come through the doors..."

I ignored her, Bernie, and Skinner and the flood of questions from the crowd of reporters that had gathered during my statement. I turned and walked back toward the church. Skinner caught up with me in a couple of strides and put his big hand on my injured shoulder.

"You go inside that church, Detective, and I will have your badge. You are putting Detective Dehan's life at risk, and also my men. You have done enough damage as it is! I have three injured men because of your reckless behavior. It is time for you to stand down!"

I took a fistful of his tie, pulled his face toward mine, and snarled into it.

"You listen to me, Skinner! If Detective Dehan had not risked her own life to get inside that place, we would now have a Waco standoff that could last for weeks and cost dozens of lives! She did the right thing and gave your men fair warning. Now back off! I do not take orders from you! My wife is in there, and I am going in to get her out, before your expert shows up and gets us all killed. Now get out of my face!"

I shoved him back, he staggered a couple of steps, and I continued to the entrance to the church. I pushed through the door, and the room rocked, so I had to lean on the doorjamb. Getting shot isn't like the movies. In the movies, if it doesn't hit a vital organ, you just wince and carry on. But in reality, if somebody shoves a lump of burning metal through two inches of flesh, vital organ or no vital organ, it hurts like hell and your body goes into deep shock. However tough you are.

I felt my skin go clammy and I began to feel cold. I told myself, "Not yet! Not yet!" I shoved myself off the doorjamb and made my way toward the doors at the back of the reception. I noticed for the first time that they were half-open, resting on the red carpet. I saw that one of the brass hinges had been shot off the left-hand door, and a voice in my head said, "See? That is where destructiveness leads."

I shook my head and made myself focus. I pushed through the doors and looked up at the gallery. Now there were two guys there with rifles. They were watching me, and between them, there was a roughly triangular patch of dried blood. David's, I guessed. This was one time when Goliath beat David.

I climbed the stairs, feeling as though I had taken some kind of hallucinogen. Every detail of my surroundings was intensified and yet seemed strangely surreal. I reached the gallery landing, and one of the two boys came forward.

I smiled weakly, exaggerating the way I felt, and said, "Take me to your leader."

He sneered. "Boy, you are a mess, man."

He patted my arms and under my shoulders. Then knelt to pat my legs.

I said, "I'm in shock, it will wear off. What's your name?"

He glanced up, momentarily distracted. "Joshua. What's it to you?" He slid his hands down my legs, predictably avoiding my crotch. The warriors of Christ don't touch other guys' crotches.

I said, "Take me to Jeremiah, Joshua. I have good news for him."

He led me through the doors and into the chapel. Nothing much had changed. Dehan was still lying on the altar stone, there were three boys sitting on the steps, watching us, and there were two holding loosely onto Dehan where she lay.

Joshua shouted, "Where is the Elder Brother? This one says he has good news."

A kid sitting on the step called back, "He doesn't know what good news is!" and they all laughed like he'd said something really funny.

At that point, Jeremiah emerged from the apse and came

around toward the altar. "I have been watching you on the TV, boy. I have to say that I admire your guts. It is a shame that you are a sinner and a deviant, or I would welcome you into the fold. Are you willing to repent?"

"Will it save the life of my wife if I do?"

He sighed noisily and looked up at the ceiling of his church. "Oh, Father! Why does he not show such devotion to his Lord, but to a whoring Jewess?"

I snarled at him, "You watch your tongue, Jeremiah. I have good news for you, but if I begin to think that there is no way to save my wife, things might start to change."

He stared at me for a long moment. While he did that, I moved over to one of the pews, in a not-so-exaggerated show of weakness, and lowered myself onto the seat. I could see his cunning, pale eyes weighing up all the odds.

In the end, he just said, "Speak!"

"Like I said, I have good news for you. But you don't get a damn word of it until you take my wife off that slab of stone, take out the gag, and cut the ropes."

"You must be out of . . ."

I cut across him and bellowed, "That is final! No deal!"

I heard the echo of my voice fade under the vaulted ceiling. He jerked his head at the boys. "Cut her loose, but not her hands. That bitch is dangerous."

He waited, eyeing me with half a smile, waiting to see if I would react. It was what I had expected him to do, so I didn't react. They lowered Dehan from the slab and cut all her bonds except the ones on her wrists. They took the gag from her mouth, and the torrent of obscenities that spilled from her mouth was unprintable.

I smiled at her. "Hi, honey."

There was a darkness to her eyes and a curl to her lip. "Your shoulder okay?"

She knew what I meant when I said, "It'll do."

They led her to a pew, where she sat, and Jeremiah asked, "So what's this good news?"

"You got your money."

He shook his head. "Bullshit. It's too fast."

I shook my head back at him. "I have a friend at NBC. Jane Harrison, she's a producer." I sighed. "This whole media circus was her idea," I lied. "She's been after us to agree to a reality show for over a year, Chief Newman is on board with it. As soon as she heard about this, she made the call."

His face lit up. "I knew it!"

"But there is a condition."

His face twisted into a scowl. "What condition?"

"They arrange everything, they square it with the cops—and believe me, they have the power, the lawyers, and the connections to do that—they pay you half now and the other half when we get back alive." He hesitated, and I made a face of exhausted irony. "She knows the consequences of crossing you, Jeremiah. She wants to make TV, she doesn't want to spend the rest of her goddamn life looking over her shoulder." He grunted, and I went on, "There is also a further option. They'll fly out to Mexico to discuss it with you. You, Dehan, and I get points. You know what that means?"

He frowned and shook his head. "Points?"

"Yeah, it's like royalties, but in film and TV. You get a percentage of the net proceeds. So the Brotherhood gets a lump sum of ten million bucks, but you get a percentage of the net proceeds of the show, plus any spin-offs and follow-ups. It's a sweet deal."

The conversation was about as surreal as any I had ever had or imagined having. I waited while he rubbed his chin and glanced at the various statues of Christ the Avenger he had standing around. His face said his Christ had swung this for him and he smiled. "All right, Stone. I said I admired you. You are a singular man. Perhaps, after all, you are a blind servant of the Lord, yet to see the light. Fine, we have a deal. So how do we proceed?"

I drew breath to talk, but he hadn't finished.

"I'll tell you how we proceed. The cops pull back, and the TV trucks form a barrier between us and the cops. We'll need three cars lined up outside, no driver, full tanks. The TV trucks will escort us to the airport, naturally NBC will have first choice of position. Tell her that. At the airport, there will be a jet waiting, with sufficient fuel to take us to Mexico . . ." He paced away toward the altar. "I also need an undertaking from the FBI that we will be immune from prosecution, so that there is no subsequent threat of extradition."

I pointed to my jacket pocket. "I'm going to get my cell to call AD Skinner. Don't shoot me. Your boy Joshua already frisked me. We cool?"

He nodded, and I dialed Bernie.

"Stone! What the hell . . . ?"

"Shut up, Bernie. He has accepted the terms. Tell Jane we need the money in cash within the hour. Now you listen really carefully, Bernie, because Dehan's life is on the line, and I do not want any fuckups."

"What? Who the hell is Jane?"

"That is not important right now. Listen to me! Tell Skinner to have the cops pull back. The TV trucks are to form a barrier between you and us, and NBC are to have preferential position . . ."

"Are you out of your mind?"

I shouted, "Shut up, Bernie! Just listen for once in your goddamn life!"

If there was one thing Bernie did in life, it was listen, and he knew that I knew that. So when I told him to listen, for once in his life, he knew that right then, he had to really listen. And he did.

"Okay, pal. I'm listening."

I stood and paced away from the altar toward the back of the church.

"We'll need three cars lined up outside, no driver, full tanks.

You got that? The TV trucks will escort us to the airport. NBC will have first choice of position. Tell Jane that. At the airport, there will be a jet waiting, with sufficient fuel to take us to Mexico. And we need an undertaking from the FBI that Jeremiah and his boys will be immune from prosecution. The Mexican authorities need to know that."

There was a moment's silence while he tried to figure out what I was really telling him. I hadn't told him anything yet, but now I shook my head and shouted again. "No! You tell that damned asshole to cool down. Do not enter this building! Goddamn it! Put Skinner on the line!"

I paused, and a moment later, Skinner's voice snapped, "What the hell is going on, Stone?"

"Shut the fuck up and listen to me, Skinner! If you send your men in here with flash-bangs and their damned guns blazing, everyone is going to die! Do you understand me? My wife, me, and all your goddamn men! You will follow the deal that has been made, and you will not—I repeat not—enter this building! Do you understand me?"

There was a moment of silence. Then he said, "Can I speak?"

"Yes!"

"I am understanding the opposite of what you are telling me."

I sighed noisily with relief. "Well, it's about goddamn time, Skinner! Dehan is safe for now, but you had better shift your ass, pal, because we are running out of time."

I hung up and looked past Joshua at Jeremiah, where he was standing by the altar steps.

"The money is on its way, five million bucks in a suitcase, and the cars are being fueled as we speak." While I was speaking, I put the cell in my left hand and thumbed Dehan's speed dial. With my right hand, I reached down under my shirt and into my crotch. Joshua had already frisked me, we'd established that, so the gesture drew more frowns than alarm. And just when they might have got alarmed, Dehan's cell rang, and they all looked at her. I pulled Bernie's Glock from my pants, placed it within six inches of Joshua's head, and squeezed the trigger.

The impact of the 9mm slug lifted him onto his toes, and a nauseating fountain of red-and-black spray erupted from his forehead. But I had no time to react. I knew I had three seconds maximum to seize the initiative, and there was just one thing I could do to achieve that. As Joshua fell, I aimed past him and plugged two slugs through Jeremiah's heart.

Dehan and I could have died in the next seconds as I ran toward her. Three of the remaining five boys were screaming in sheer horror as they watched their Elder Brother keel over onto the altar steps, but the other two, flushed with rage, were raising their weapons and lining me up. I knew I might take one, but not both.

Thankfully, AD Skinner timed it about right. There was a loud explosion, a scream from the gallery, and the dry rattle of automatic rifle fire. I had been expecting it, they hadn't, and they hesitated for a second. It was all I needed to shoot the two of them in the chest, grab Dehan, and drag her along the front pew and into the cover of the side aisle. I dragged her to the floor and lay on top of her, muffling her shouts of protest.

The door to the chapel exploded; there was a collective cry of fearful surrender and bellowing voices roaring, "Get down! On your bellies! Now! Hands behind your heads! Now! Now! Now!"

More orders were barked, and then there was Bernie, hollering our names. "Stone! For Christ's sake, Stone! Where are you? Carmen, goddamn it!"

I eased myself off her and smiled into her ragged, pale face. She smiled back and started to giggle. "You asshole," she said affectionately. "You total, insane asshole!" She looped her bound wrists over my head and drew me to her. The kiss was long and totally inappropriate in the setting and the circumstances.

After a moment, I heard Bernie's voice just a couple of pews away. "Oh, Jesus, what now? You couldn't wait?"

I shook my head, with my face still attached to Dehan's. "Mh-mh," I said, "mh-mh!"

NINETEEN

The center of Belfast resembled a war zone. Resistance from some of the members of the Brotherhood had been surprisingly intense. They were not huge in number, but they were well armed and, above all, fanatical in their belief in their divine protection. Sadly for them, their divine protection seemed to be under review at the time, and, aside from the four killed at the church, half a dozen more were killed in firefights around the city, and a dozen more were arrested.

Four men in their thirties were detained attempting to escape the city in a car. They drew weapons and engaged the police, and all four were shot dead.

As the sky began to fade to gray in the east and Dehan and I sat in the back of an ambulance being tended by paramedics brought in by the FBI, reports began to reach us that federal and state units had raided City Hall, the police station, and a number of private properties. There had been arrests, many of them cops and City Hall employees, though the number was not yet clear. The National Guard had been called in, and there was a curfew in place. The citizens were, apparently, stunned, but the small city of Belfast was now quiet and peaceful, and the citizens were going about their daily business, bemused rather than outraged.

The bureau's specialists had set up camp in the offices and archives of the police station, the courthouse, City Hall, and the Church of the Sacred Brotherhood, and were going through every scrap of paper they could find. But it soon became clear that while the official government buildings held practically nothing, the archives in the vault of the church were a gold mine. All the minutes of all the meetings held since 1649 were there, including those in which the reinstitution of the Hearings of Sentence of Death and Decrees of Execution were decided, twenty years earlier, when Jeremiah Rose was appointed Elder Brother.

The minutes of the Council sitting in Closed Session also emerged, and there, at the meeting of September 1, 2010, after hearing the pleas of her brother, Captain Ewan Jones, to stay their hand, the Council agreed to sentence her to death, and ordered the execution of that order three weeks later.

We now sat in that vault, in a small office that acted as an antechamber. Dehan sat behind the desk, reading the two documents that sentenced Sally to death and ordered the execution of that sentence. She read them carefully while Bernie and I watched her in silence.

Bernie looked up and smiled at me. "How's the shoulder?"

"I'll live, but I am going to need at least a month sitting on a beach somewhere eating sirloin steak and drinking fine wine."

"You've earned it, both of you. That was some pretty hot shit you pulled back there. You were lucky it came off."

Dehan didn't look up. She was photographing the orders with her phone. He drew breath, probably to tell her she couldn't do that, but she growled, "Luck had nothing to do with it, Bernie. Hours of relentless training, feline reflexes, and a profoundly predatory nature. Luck is for pussies."

Then she smiled and stood. "I'm taking my man home to nurse his wounds and feed him very dry martinis. If you need us, you know where to find us."

"Jesus! Go, for God's sake, before I start throwing up. You know what my wife does when I get wounded?"

I laughed. "No, what does she do, Bernie?"

"Nothing! I never get wounded! Now go! Jesus!"

We left. We climbed the steps up to the ground floor of the church and then hobbled out into the gray, damp dawn. It had, at least, stopped raining, and only slight spits of rain fell from the broken clouds. We crossed the yard out onto the sidewalk. There were only a couple of cop cars now, and the crime scene van. The ambulances had left, taking the dead and the wounded with them. Above our heads, in the autumn trees, birds were singing desultory songs about the fall. I leaned painfully on the damp roof of the Jaguar and looked at Dehan. She held out her hands, cupped to receive the keys. I tossed them to her, and she opened the door.

"You are serious," I said.

"Yup." She smiled and climbed in.

I climbed in after her and slammed the door. "It's a six-hour drive. You're exhausted. I'm exhausted. We need to sleep."

"Plenty of time to sleep when you're dead." She shoved the key in the ignition, turned it, and the big, old engine growled into life. "If I start to flag on the way, we'll pull over into a motel for a couple of hours."

"Yeah." I nodded. "That's a crazy, novel idea."

"I'm hyped. Quit griping and rest your wound."

I did. I quit griping, closed my eyes, and allowed the painkillers they had given me to take effect. It didn't take long. Pretty soon, the movement of the car, the sheer exhaustion, and the pills worked their combined magic, and I was unconscious. I came to a couple of times, saw the gray skies, the drizzle on the windshield, and Dehan glancing a smile at me, and went back to sleep again.

When I awoke properly, it was because Dehan was shaking me gently.

"Hey, big guy, we're here and it's lunchtime. Wake up."

I opened my eyes, and for a while, the landscape did not seem to have changed much. Then it dawned on me that we were in a driveway, surrounded by trees, and after that, I realized it was Leon Cohen's driveway.

"What the hell are we doing here, Dehan?"

She shrugged. "I called him from the car to tell him the case had been solved, and he asked us to drop by and fill him in."

I narrowed my eyes at her. "What? You taken a shine to this guy or what?"

"Don't be stupid, Stone. He's a nice guy, he helped us, and he likes your car."

"I'm wounded! You were going to take me home and feed me very dry martinis. Now we're in Long Island talking to nice, rich guys. I am not happy."

"Come on! This will take ten minutes. Then I'll take you home and make you wish you were not wounded. I promise."

I sulked and clambered one-handed out of the Jag. Leon was waiting at the door, looking debonair and smiling at Dehan with uncertain eyes.

"My goodness! You look exhausted. I mean"—he gestured at Dehan—"beautiful as ever, but exhausted." He frowned at me. "And, my word! Detective Stone! Are you injured? Do you need a doctor?"

I thought of all sorts of bitter responses but kept them to myself and smiled. "I'll live, thanks."

"Come on inside. Are you on duty? Can I offer you a drink?"

"Nothing for Detective Dehan, thanks. She's driving. But if you have a Bushmills, I'll have a double, no ice."

We were in his large hall, and he was gesturing us toward the drawing room, but Dehan stopped dead in her tracks and gave him a mischievous smile. "Can I be really cheeky?"

He gave her a smile that was meant for her and intended to exclude me. "Please do."

"It has been on my mind since we saw you last, and I just know it would give Stone a lot of pleasure. Could we see your cars while I fill you in on what happened? I mean, we have confessions, documentary proof, the works! The two of them were killed because *she* strayed from the religious sect she was born into. It's the craziest damn thing I ever saw."

He smiled and spread his hands. "Of course, how could I say no when you have been kind enough to come out of your way." He rang a bell. "And both so exhausted. If I'd had any idea . . ."

A door opened, and his French maid stepped out. "Michelle, bring a bottle of Bushmills, two tumblers, and some ice to the museum." Then he turned back to us. "This way, please."

We followed him across a damp lawn toward a series of coach houses and stables set in a gravel courtyard. There were no windows, and two of the stable doors had been replaced by roller blinds. He reached in his pocket, and a second later, the blinds started to roll up, making a loud clattering in the quiet, early afternoon. The lights came on automatically as we stepped through the door.

We were in a long, simple, whitewashed nave with a bare, wooden A-frame structure supporting a gabled roof. But the display, scattered around the terra-cotta tiled floor, was stunning. There was a 1957 Ferrari Dino in fire-engine red, there was a 1960 Jaguar XK Roadster, a 1965 Lamborghini 350 GT, a crimson Corvette Stingray sitting beside a mint E-Type Jaguar, right-hand drive. There were others: a cream Alfa Romeo Giulietta, an AC Cobra . . . and an empty space.

Dehan shook her head. "This is wild," she said. "Just crazy. I mean, what is this worth?"

He shrugged. "Financially, there are probably fifteen million dollars' worth of cars here, but their value goes well beyond that. These are cars from an era where men designed cars to satisfy their dreams, to fulfill ambitions that went far beyond money. These cars represent the dying glimmer of an era when human beings aspired to more than merely belonging to the hive, and plugging into the Hive Mind. The sixties was a decade of dreams, and these cars epitomized those dreams."

She pointed at the empty space. "And this was the space reserved for the Mustang, huh?"

He nodded. "Yes, and it still is. I trust it will be returned before very long."

She wagged a finger at him. "I believe you are right." She looked around for a moment, then started walking toward the Alfa Romeo that was parked against the far wall on the right. Dehan spoke over her shoulder as she walked.

"You know, Leon, you are a smart guy. Like, collecting these cars. Right here, you have fifteen million bucks that do not represent a taxable income, am I right? But you are not blinded by their economic value . . ."

She ignored the Alfa and leaned right up close to the wall, till she was less than an inch away. "You, being deep and sensitive, and attuned to higher things, perceive the deeper value of the thing, in the context of its social setting. It takes intelligence to do that."

Now she was staring up into the rafters, where the wall didn't quite reach the roof. She stared suddenly at Leon, with no expression. I was trying to think who she reminded me of in my slightly feverish state, and I settled on Colombo. She was talking again.

"I am supposed to be telling you what happened, and instead I am flattering you with compliments. What am I like?" She pointed in the general direction of the house. "You'll see it on the news if you didn't see it already. It was a war zone. The Feds and the state police took over the police station, City Hall—can you believe it? And the Church of the Sacred Brotherhood of Christ. That's who did it. It's in the records. You don't mind me looking around?"

He forced a smile. "Please help yourself, though shortly I must . . ."

He glanced at his watch and then gasped as she jumped on the hood of the Alfa and from there jumped up and took hold of the A-frame holding up the ceiling. There, she swung a moment and pulled herself up till she was sitting astride it.

"It's a cool view from up here. You could take some handsome photographs. You know, speaking of photographs, back in the day, when you and Gus and Sally were all pals, you must have made him an offer for the Mustang."

He stared but didn't answer. There was just utter stillness in the museum. Her voice, when it came again from up in the rafters, was startling.

"See, we had the photograph of him and Sally sitting on the damned thing, with McQueen's personalized plates. And when I checked with Detective del Rio, it was clear they were the same damned plates and the same car. So that got me thinking, like, what are the chances that your car, of all people, *your car* should go missing the day after we start investigating Sally's murder? And then . . ." She pulled up a leg and rested the ankle on the wood. "It turns out that the guy who owned the car before you was not just Sally's boyfriend, but was murdered the very night that *she* was killed! Now, that is too much coincidence in *anybody's* book, right? But in a cop's book, it is just not possible. So I got to thinking and turning it over and pulling it inside out and I just could not make head nor tail of it. And all the while, the evidence against the Brotherhood was just mounting up. I was about to throw in the towel and put it down to a freakish example of synchronicity when you said something."

He swallowed, but that was the only response he made.

She pointed at him, like a sniper taking aim. "You know what you said, Leon? You said that you didn't remember Gus' name. And I don't care how forgetful you are, you . . ." She jabbed her finger at him. "*You* would remember the name of the guy who sold you the 1965 Mustang Fastback once owned by Steve McQueen." She paused.

He shook his head and gave a tight laugh. "That's ridiculous."

"Is it? But you know what isn't ridiculous? Nobody, not even Maya Hernandez, Sally's pal, knew that Gus had been murdered that night. But you did. Even the cops at the Forty-Third hadn't put that two and two together. But you knew. How come you knew?"

"I . . ." He shrugged and shook his head again. "This is ridiculous. It was public knowledge. I can't explain your ignorance!"

"Maybe you can explain something else, then."

"What?"

I was wondering the same thing. I was also wondering why she was sitting in the rafters. She pointed back at the wall and said, "Why your 1965 Mustang Fastback, once the property of Steve McQueen, is sitting behind that wall."

He covered his face with his hands. I looked at him and smiled. When I looked back at Dehan, she was standing on the rafter, taking a big step onto the top of the wall.

She had to hunker down to fit through the gap, but she called to me, "There's a door. I figure we have probable cause, Stone. Kick it in or something, will you?"

I pulled my weapon and showed it to him. "Shall we use my key or yours?"

Two minutes later, we opened the door and stepped in. The Mustang was there, in a space about twenty feet square. Dehan was not visible, but the trunk was open, and I could hear her.

She peered around and held up a paper napkin in a plastic evidence bag. I could see there was writing scrawled on it. Leon leaned against the wall and slid down to the floor, his face buried in his hands.

Dehan switched her gaze to me. "Picture a guy who gets away with a nearly perfect murder. The only weakness in it is that, instead of the case being closed and the wrong guy getting convicted, the case goes cold. Then, ten years later, it is reopened, but it is reopened in a blaze of national publicity, and the killer hears about it. Central to the whole case, though nobody knows it at the time, is the 1965 Mustang that our killer was desperate to buy."

I stared down at Leon, then over at Dehan. "I don't understand how killing Sally and cutting off her hands and feet ties in with this damned car." There was a chair by the door, and I lowered myself onto it.

She waved the napkin at me. "You know what this is?"

"Of course not, Dehan."

"It's what Maya was telling us about. It was what made that last night, in Leon's words, 'wild.' It is a will. Gus had somehow picked up the Mustang from some dealer . . ."

Leon spoke into his hands. "It was at an auction, and the ignorant bastards had no idea what the car was, despite the damned plates. I, like the damned fool that I am, was the one who told him what he had."

"So Leon here was crazy trying to buy it from Gus. But Gus was having fun putting down the Ivy League kid, making him beg and making himself look smart for his lady Sally. That was bad enough, but that last night, when they had what Maya called the ruckus, was when Gus wrote this. A legal document leaving his precious Mustang to Sally."

"Holy cow," I said and turned to Leon. "So you went and killed Gus, and then you went and killed her? It was a damned car, for Christ's sake!"

He was shaking his head, but Dehan was talking again. "It was more than a damned car, Stone. It was maybe a million bucks' worth of car at auction. But I don't think Leon killed them both. Two things make me think it played out different. First off, Leon might have wanted to kill Gus, but he would be very aware that killing Gus would hand the car on a platter to Sally. To conceive of a double murder would be pushing it for a first-time killer. Second, the MO. The MO is totally different. In fact, the MO is consistent with the assassination methods of the Brotherhood."

I nodded. "Jesus . . . !"

"We will find out when the interrogations start, but two gets you twenty, Stone, that Captain Jones was one of the Brotherhood's hit men . . ."

"But we know he didn't hit Gus."

"I know, but I think his sister did."

"What?"

"She's right. I was raging mad that night. I had wanted Sally for a long time. I had paid for her a hundred times over, and that shit Gus could have her for the price of a beer. I was sick of both of them, and when they played that stunt with the car—a car that meant *nothing* to them and everything to me—I went crazy. I followed Sally home. I don't know what I was planning to do, but I was going to make her give me something . . ."

I said, "You were planning to rape her?"

"Maybe, but I didn't. Before I could build up the nerve to do anything, she came out again, got in her car, and went to Gus' place. She was up there awhile, not long, then came running down, got in her car, and went home. I was fascinated. I had a strange, bad feeling. I went up and found him. She'd shot him through the heart. Cold as ice. I looked for the will, but it was gone. That proved it to me. He had a big hunting knife hanging on the wall. I don't think I had formed the intention yet, but I might have. I went back to her place. The bitch was asleep. She'd just killed a guy, and all her clothes were neatly folded and she was asleep, like nothing had happened. In that moment, I hated her. I stabbed her in the heart and then I went a bit crazy. I cut off her hands for being a thief, and I cut off her feet to symbolize the fact that she could not run away from what she had done. Then I took her paper napkin will, and I left."

Dehan finished off for him. "After that, you bought the car at auction when Gus' estate was sold off to cover his business debts."

He dropped his hands and nodded at her. "That's correct. Now I guess my hands and my feet will be cut off, but only metaphorically."

She hauled a box out of the trunk and showed it to him. "This them?"

"Yeah, I kept them as trophies. I had, after all, bested her at her own game."

I ran my fingers through my hair. "So Sally killed Gus so she could get the car . . ."

Dehan said, "A million bucks' worth of car!"

"And then you killed Sally..."

Dehan cut in again. "Out of sexual revenge, and for the car." She sighed and looked at him. "Leon Cohen, I am placing you under arrest for the murder of Sally Jones..."

EPILOGUE

The fire was crackling and spitting sparks out onto the hearth. Outside, the rain was pattering against the glass and tap-tapping on the windowsill. I was stretched out on the sofa with a very large, very dry Martini in my hand. Dehan was in the kitchen, and the smell of seared sirloin was wafting benevolently on the air.

"What I still don't get," I said, "is why you continued to suspect Leon even after we got the documents from the Brotherhood stating that Sally was to be executed."

"Stone, you were wounded, exhausted, and the woman of your dreams had almost been sacrificed on a stone altar, so it is understandable that you did not immediately see it."

"See *what* exactly, Woman of my Dreams?"

"Well, a couple of things." There was a wild hiss as she turned the steak over. "For a start, there was no sentence of death or order of execution for Gus. Which meant there was somebody else at work here. Also, when we spoke to Maya and she told me about the paper napkin, I had already nailed the fact that it was all about *how* Leon got the car from Gus. I was totally clear that that transfer of property was central to the murder. But why kill Sally? Gus was the guy with the car. So there could be only one explanation. Before the car reached Leon, it passed through Sally. That paper napkin that annoyed Leon so much was the explanation."

"That's brilliant."

"And there was one other thing. While you and Bernie were talking about how lucky we were, I was scouring the death warrants. They said nothing at all about dismemberment. Which convinced me that she had been killed before the Brotherhood were able to execute the warrants."

"Brilliant. You are a very brilliant woman, Dehan. And that makes you very desirable."

I said it sleepily, with my eyes closed.

I heard the plates clatter on the table and the comfortable gurgle of red wine being spilled into a glass.

"Well, come and desire this, big guy. And then we have an appointment."

I raised my head and looked at her in dismay. "We have a what?"

"An appointment, with each other. I am going to make you wish you were not injured, remember?"

She winked, and I smiled. Then I got up and went to the table, amazed, not for the first or the last time, at my luck.

Don't miss A CHRISTMAS KILLING. The riveting sequel in the Dead Cold Mystery series.

Scan the QR code below to purchase A CHRISTMAS KILLING.

Or go to: righthouse.com/a-christmas-killing

NOTE: flip to the very end to read an exclusive sneak peak...

DON'T MISS ANYTHING!

If you want to stay up to date on all new releases in this series, with this author, or with any of our new deals, you can do so by joining our newsletters below.

In addition, you will immediately gain access to our entire *Right House VIP Library*, which includes many riveting Mystery and Thriller novels for your enjoyment!

righthouse.com/email

(Easy to unsubscribe. No spam. Ever.)

ALSO BY BLAKE BANNER

Up to date books can be found at:
www.righthouse.com/blake-banner

ROGUE THRILLERS
Gates of Hell (Book 1)
Hell's Fury (Book 2)

ALEX MASON THRILLERS
Odin (Book 1)
Ice Cold Spy (Book 2)
Mason's Law (Book 3)
Assets and Liabilities (Book 4)
Russian Roulette (Book 5)
Executive Order (Book 6)
Dead Man Talking (Book 7)
All The King's Men (Book 8)
Flashpoint (Book 9)
Brotherhood of the Goat (Book 10)
Dead Hot (Book 11)
Blood on Megiddo (Book 12)
Son of Hell (Book 13)

HARRY BAUER THRILLER SERIES
Dead of Night (Book 1)
Dying Breath (Book 2)
The Einstaat Brief (Book 3)
Quantum Kill (Book 4)
Immortal Hate (Book 5)
The Silent Blade (Book 6)
LA: Wild Justice (Book 7)

Breath of Hell (Book 8)
Invisible Evil (Book 9)
The Shadow of Ukupacha (Book 10)
Sweet Razor Cut (Book 11)
Blood of the Innocent (Book 12)
Blood on Balthazar (Book 13)
Simple Kill (Book 14)
Riding The Devil (Book 15)
The Unavenged (Book 16)
The Devil's Vengeance (Book 17)
Bloody Retribution (Book 18)
Rogue Kill (Book 19)
Blood for Blood (Book 20)

DEAD COLD MYSTERY SERIES
An Ace and a Pair (Book 1)
Two Bare Arms (Book 2)
Garden of the Damned (Book 3)
Let Us Prey (Book 4)
The Sins of the Father (Book 5)
Strange and Sinister Path (Book 6)
The Heart to Kill (Book 7)
Unnatural Murder (Book 8)
Fire from Heaven (Book 9)
To Kill Upon A Kiss (Book 10)
Murder Most Scottish (Book 11)
The Butcher of Whitechapel (Book 12)
Little Dead Riding Hood (Book 13)
Trick or Treat (Book 14)
Blood Into Wine (Book 15)
Jack In The Box (Book 16)
The Fall Moon (Book 17)
Blood In Babylon (Book 18)
Death In Dexter (Book 19)
Mustang Sally (Book 20)

A Christmas Killing (Book 21)
Mommy's Little Killer (Book 22)
Bleed Out (Book 23)
Dead and Buried (Book 24)
In Hot Blood (Book 25)
Fallen Angels (Book 26)
Knife Edge (Book 27)
Along Came A Spider (Book 28)
Cold Blood (Book 29)
Curtain Call (Book 30)

THE OMEGA SERIES
Dawn of the Hunter (Book 1)
Double Edged Blade (Book 2)
The Storm (Book 3)
The Hand of War (Book 4)
A Harvest of Blood (Book 5)
To Rule in Hell (Book 6)
Kill: One (Book 7)
Powder Burn (Book 8)
Kill: Two (Book 9)
Unleashed (Book 10)
The Omicron Kill (Book 11)
9mm Justice (Book 12)
Kill: Four (Book 13)
Death In Freedom (Book 14)
Endgame (Book 15)

ABOUT US

Right House is an independent publisher created by authors for readers. We specialize in Action, Thriller, Mystery, and Crime novels.

If you enjoyed this novel, then there is a good chance you will like what else we have to offer! Please stay up to date by using any of the links below.

Join our mailing lists to stay up to date -->
righthouse.com/email
Visit our website --> righthouse.com
Contact us --> contact@righthouse.com

facebook.com/righthousebooks
x.com/righthousebooks
instagram.com/righthousebooks

EXCLUSIVE SNEAK PEAK OF...

A CHRISTMAS KILLING

CHAPTER 1

"Lilith was a bit dumb. Her father thought she was smart, but I always thought she was kind of dumb. I know, maybe a mother shouldn't talk like that about her daughter, but what can I tell you but the truth? She wasn't mentally retarded, or like some kids you see who walk around with their mouths open all the time. You know the kind of thing? She wasn't like that. She was bright and fun and always laughing and..."

Lilith's mother paused to shake her head and suppress a sob. I watched a tear creep along her lower eyelid and pause before spilling down her cheek toward the corner of her mouth. The Christmas tree in the corner twinkled sadly.

"Affectionate," she said at last and nodded, like she'd chosen a particularly good word. "She was real affectionate with everyone. She was also a bit narcissistic. She hid it because she was so sweet and everybody loved her. But if ever you had a conversation *with* Lilith, the conversation was *about* Lilith." I drew breath to ask a question, but she waved it away like an annoying fly. "You could start a conversation about anything. Before thirty seconds were up, she'd say, 'For *me* . . .' and turn it around so you were talking about her."

Dehan cleared her throat. "We are particularly interested in . . ."

Lilith's mother spoke on. "My mother died. Lilith never knew my mother. She cried nonstop for a week, about the fact that I never let her meet her grandmother. In the end everyone was saying, 'Poor Lilith. She never knew her grandmother. Now she's dead. It must be so hard for her.' I just lost my mother, but screw me." She sighed. "But sweet. Sweet as a sugarplum."

Her eyes strayed to a plum cake that was sitting on a side table, fenced in by sprigs of holly. I said, "So she had a lot of friends?"

"Oh, plenty. Everyone at her job adored her. She was training to be a nurse, you know, but volunteered at a thrift store. You know how it is, Detective Stone, when you look like a Playboy pinup and have the personality of a dumb blonde, you've got a hundred and one friends, and they're all guys who want to get inside your panties. But *are* they friends?"

She spread her hands and nodded slowly, using her whole body. It was meant to be an expression of worldly wisdom. Instead it made her look like a seagull doing a balancing act on a buoy in rough seas.

"Do any of those friends stand out?"

"*All* of them stand out—for the lascivious hypocrites that they were. When they wanted to screw her, they were lining up like dildos on parade! But when she was being killed, where were they?"

Dehan leaned forward with narrowed eyes. "That," she said, "is what we are trying to find out. So what we need to know is, who?"

"Who?"

"Who?" Dehan nodded elaborately, and I couldn't resist asking, "Who?"

She ignored me and spoke to Lilith's mother. "Mrs. Jones, right now, those hundreds of lined-up dildos are just an anonymous mass of latex." Mrs. Jones frowned at the image. Dehan went on regardless. "That doesn't help us. We need a lot more than just general, anonymous latex."

"More than latex?"

"More information. We need to know how many men were lining up for Lilith's favors, we need to know their names and addresses..."

Mrs. Jones shrugged. "I don't know..."

Dehan reached out her hand and gripped Mrs. Jones' wrist. "That's okay. But think for a moment—wasn't there one who stood out from the rest? Wasn't there one who was a little more keen, called her more often, tried harder than the others...?"

"You mean like a boyfriend?"

Dehan nodded. "For example."

"Well, she *had* a boyfriend."

Dehan sighed. There was a hint of a groan in the sigh. "You didn't mention this in the original police investigation?"

"I was extremely upset. So I don't honestly know *what* I told that detective. He was *fat* and I did not like talking to him. Also, I never met her boyfriend."

I frowned and scratched my chin at the same time. "You never met her boyfriend?"

The coal glowed in the grate, and outside the wind rattled the window and threatened snow. The tinsel on the tree shivered. Mrs. Jones shook her head, and for a moment I thought that was all the answer I was going to get. But finally she said, "Lilith was a strange girl. To anyone who met her she was an angel, sweet, always laughing and kind and gentle. But at home she could be..." She nodded several times before saying, "...*cutting*."

Dehan echoed her, "Cutting..."

"Cutting, like a knife. She told me she didn't want her boyfriend to meet me because I was weird. Weird, me. I have worked my fingers to the bone to put a roof over her head and a plate of food on the table, because her father, may he rot in hell, died on us when she was no more than two years old. Can you believe that? Dying like that? And she says I am *weird*!"

Dehan smiled with her mouth. Her eyes said something that was not infused with the Christmas spirit. "So what *do* you know about her boyfriend, aside from the fact that she had one?"

"Uh... nothing?"

Dehan turned to me with a face like a summons. I gave my head a small, one-sided shake and drew breath to speak to Mrs. Jones. She preempted me.

"Then there was Ern."

"Ern?"

"Ern was Pat's brother. I told your fat detective about him. He's fat too, like Pat. They were all fat. They would have been good friends, getting fat together."

"About Ern and Lilith...?"

"He was obsessed with her: O-B-S-E-S-T! When he came to visit Pat and Cyril, which was often, he could never stay in his sister's house. He just *had* to come over here and start sniffing around Lilith's skirts."

I glanced at Dehan. She gave a fractional shrug. Brother Ernest had been mentioned in Mo's report, but nothing about his obsession with Lilith. I allowed my eyebrows to say I was interested and asked her, "What do you mean exactly by the phrase, 'sniffing around her skirts'?"

Mrs. Jones looked at Dehan and smiled maliciously. "That's cute," she said. "A homicide cop in the Bronx who has managed to hold on to his innocence."

Dehan's smile was dangerous. "Oh, I think he knows what the expression means, Mrs. Jones, but I think my partner would like to know what Ern used to do. What was his behavior? What makes you say that he was 'sniffing around her skirts.' Precisely, what did he do?"

"I would offer you eggnog, but I am keeping it for my family when they come and visit."

"Thanks, we're on duty. His behavior?"

"He's a mental retard. He's smart enough to tie his shoes and do a simple job. I don't know what he does, but it's simple, you can be sure of that." Her lip curled into an unpleasant smile. "Maybe he's a janitor or something. Anyhow, he used to come 'round and sit where you're sitting"—she pointed at me—"and just kind of gawp at Lilith, and ask her stupid questions . . ."

Dehan asked, "What kind of questions?"

Mrs. Jones sighed. "Like, did she have a boyfriend, was she ever going to get married, would she go to the cinema with him. Once he asked her if she would marry him, another time he asked her what color her panties were. That time I got mad and threw him out. After that he used to come and stand at the fence looking in, and Lilith felt sorry for him—or loved the attention, take your pick—and she'd go and stand talking to him over the fence. So I had to let him come in again."

I nodded and cleared my throat. "So, was he here that Christmas Eve when Lilith was murdered?"

"Yup."

I waited. She watched me wait. Dehan said, "You want to tell us about that?"

She shrugged. "What do you want me to tell you? I already told the detective the first time he came 'round, a year ago. Ern came 'round Christmas morning. He wanted to show us some stupid sweater and socks he'd got from his sister and her husband. The sweater was big, fat horizontal red-and-white stripes with reindeer and stupid stuff like that on it. All the noses and the antlers were in relief, you know the kind of thing. The socks matched the sweater. They were both nauseating, but like I said, he was kind of stupid and he liked them, and he wanted to show Lilith."

"What sort of time was that?"

"Just around the time you're most busy in the kitchen preparing the Christmas dinner, about ten or eleven in the morning. He turns up at the door looking more like something out of Halloween than Christmas morning, with that goofy face, saying, 'Hellow, Mrs. Jones, is Lilith in? I want to show her my pwesents.' I called her, I said, 'Lilith, it's your boyfriend!'

You should have seen his face. It was redder than his damn sweater."

Dehan smiled. "You were making Christmas dinner for you and Lilith? Nobody else?"

"Just me and her. There was nobody else. I told her to bring her boyfriend for Christmas, to meet her mom. But she told me, 'No, I don't want him to meet you, Mom, because you're weird.' Weird, me. Me, weird. I ask you directly, Detective Stone, do I look weird to you?"

Aside from her peroxide hair and her very red lips, she did not look especially weird, but it was a conversation I was not keen to get into. I gave her a sympathetic smile instead and asked her, "So it was just the two of you for Christmas dinner, and then Ern showed up. What happened next?"

"What happened next? Well she sat with him in the parlor while he drooled over her and I roasted a turkey, made stuffing, prepared more eggnog . . ."

"That's rough." Dehan shook her head. "I hate it when that happens. What happened after that?"

"Well, then Cyril came over to get Ern."

"Cyril was Ern's brother-in-law."

"Still is, far as I know. Little mincing mouse of a man. Humble. You know the sort. I don't hate him. He's a nice man, always polite, always helpful, but so damn humble sometimes I just want to backhand him and tell him to man up. You just don't get real men anymore, Detective Stone. My Davie, now that was a man. No BS, one hundred percent testosterone-fueled man. Now he's dead, the son of a bitch. But I see men today, with their moisturizing creams, their hair conditioners, and their pink shirts, and I fear for the future of our race. Don't you?"

"All the time. So he came over to collect Ern, and then what happened?"

She rolled her eyes and gave her peroxide hair a shake. I looked at the angel on the top of the tree, and it struck me there was something manic about the way she was staring at the ceiling.

"Well, Lilith, who just couldn't get enough male attention, started offering them eggnog and fruitcake and this and that, and I'm saying to her, 'Well, come on, honey, they have to get back and help with *their own* Christmas dinner!' Kind of hinting discreetly, but when Lilith was lapping up attention, you couldn't get through to her. She was just: 'Oh, Mom! Cyril and Ern just popped over in the spirit of the season to say hi. Least we can do is show some hospitality!' So they stayed, and we were getting closer and closer to lunchtime and I just did not know what to do!"

"Okay, stop."

She stared at me wide-eyed. Dehan arched an eyebrow at me. I raised one hand and said, "I need to be clear about this. Cyril joined Ern here and Lilith encouraged them both to stay."

"That *is* what I just said."

"Okay, let's take this one step at a time. How did Ern react to Cyril's arrival?"

"Well he didn't break open the champagne, if that's what you mean. Cyril is smart and funny. He won't prepossess you with his appearance, but he's smart and he has a real funny sense of humor. He's shy, when there's lots of people, like, but when it's just a few friends he comes out of his shell and he is real funny. So when he showed up and started stealing the scene, Ern wasn't too happy."

Dehan spoke my thoughts. "How did that manifest? What did he do?"

She shrugged. "He sulked. He sat right there on the sofa with his hands in his lap and his big fat bottom lip stuck out and stared at his knees."

"While Cyril sat and made Lilith laugh?"

"And I worked my pretty little butt off in the kitchen."

Dehan suppressed a sigh by tying her hair in a knot at the back of her neck, narrowed her eyes, and asked, "How did you get them to leave?"

"I didn't. Like I told your fat detective, I couldn't get them to leave. It was two thirty before they went. And they only went because the big battleship came and got them."

"The big battleship?"

"Patricia, Cyril's wife, Ern's sister. She looked like a Spanish galleon in full sail. She came down my path like eight sacks of angry jelly and started pounding on my door. 'Cyril Perkins! Are you in there? You come out here right this minute!' Well you should have seen Ern jump. Cyril apologized for staying so long, and Lilith saw them to the door. I came out following, wiping my hands on a tea towel."

She put her fingertips to her forehead and gave a small shake.

"I have never . . . in my life . . . *seen* such a spectacle. You would not credit it if you did not see it. She was *howling* like a dog, waving her great arms about, wobbling like three hundred pounds of aspic, and the *language*! Well, as my sainted grandmother used to say, 'I do declare! Them words would make the Devil himself blush!'"

"What," said Dehan, and narrowed her eyes again. "What was it, exactly, that she was mad about?"

"The most ridiculous thing I ever heard. She thought that Cyril and Lilith were having an affair!"

"What made her think that?"

"Blessed if I know! Lilith was very sociable, very friendly, and very affectionate, and as I may have pointed out earlier, she was a sucker for male attention. Often when she came home from work, Cyril would be in his front yard smoking his pipe and they would stop and talk. Other times she would invite him over for afternoon coffee and they'd sit and talk. He always made her laugh a lot. But he is just a timid old man with a lively sense of humor. Pat was insane to think there was anything going on. A beautiful young girl like her and an old man like him. Why, he must be sixty, and at that time, last year, she was just twenty-three. The idea is just disgusting."

I scratched my chin. "Any idea what put it in her head?"

"Sure. She's crazy. She's fat, ugly, and stupid and spends her whole day imagining her husband is out doing the kinds of things she wishes she was doing."

I grunted. Pop psychology I could come up with myself. What I needed was facts—the facts Mo had missed a year back when he took the case.

"Anything more concrete than that?"

She shook her head. "No. It was based on nothing. I mean, the man watched Lilith grow up, for heaven's sake. And as she got older, they became garden fence friends. But Pat was such a bitter, twisted, evil woman that she read wickedness into everything." She paused a moment, suddenly serious and thoughtful. "I think it had a lot more to do with Lilith and Pat than it had to do with Cyril. Lilith was young and beautiful, Pat was grotesque, and she knew she was getting old. She just hated Lilith, plain and simple."

Dehan nodded, like it made sense to her. "Did anything she say, any phrase or word, strike you as especially significant?"

"No, she said she, Lilith, was well named, called her a whore, a thief, stealing other women's husbands, a tramp, a cheap slut . . ." She shrugged, then smiled at Dehan. "Lilith was vain, a narcissist, but she didn't deserve to be called those things. She was a nice kid, a good girl."

And then the tears started to spill again, slipping down her cheeks, touched with fire and the colored sparkles of Christmas.

Mrs. Jones rose and went to the kitchen. She returned a couple of minutes later with a tray of coffee and a glass of eggnog for herself. She set them down and sat. The room was very quiet. She was gazing into her drink, biting her lip and tipping her head from side to side, as though she had found something infinitely sad in her glass of eggnog.

After a moment she gave an extremely heavy sigh and spoke.

"Cyril and Ern managed to pull her back down the road. It wasn't easy. There had been a bit of snow and the sidewalk was slippery, and she was big and struggling and screaming. I remember a few of the neighbors had come out to see what all the ruckus was about. She just ignored them and kept turning back and shouting abuse at Lilith, telling her to keep her filthy hands to herself, until they got to their house. They pushed her through the gate and up the steps and that was the last we saw of them . . . At least it was the last I saw of them."

Dehan's voice was quiet. "What do you mean by that, Mrs. Jones?"

Mrs. Jones raised her eyes to look at Dehan's face. They were full of reproach, anger, and incomprehension. "Well, Lilith saw Pat again, didn't she? Later that evening. I sent her, like I did every year, to take a Christmas supper to old Mrs. Rodriguez down on the corner of Gildersleeve. Some turkey, mashed potatoes, broccoli, Christmas pudding . . ."

She trailed off, staring at us each in turn. I waited. She spoke suddenly, and her voice was startling and loud.

"She's dead now. Mrs. Rodriguez. She was very old. She died March fourth. That was the last Christmas meal I ever sent her. Lilith went over at like four in the afternoon, and she stayed with her till about seven I guess. I don't know what time, really, but at least seven. She was good like that, kind, you know? Affectionate. So when she came back it was dark. All the windows down Pugsley Avenue had their drapes closed. All the doors were closed. Everybody was watching a movie, sleeping in front of the fire after Christmas lunch, stroking the cat, or the dogs . . ."

Her eyes were wide and unseeing, staring at the window where already the early-afternoon light was beginning to fade. She blinked and looked down at the floor. "She had dogs," she said. "Pat, two nasty little ratlike dogs, always yapping. By seven thirty I was getting worried, so just before eight I called Mrs. Rodriguez and asked to speak with Lilith. She said Lilith had gone about half an hour earlier. So I thought, maybe she'd fallen and hurt herself . . ."

The flood came again, harder this time. Her eyes were bright but glazed with tears, her nose suddenly red, as though from a cold. Her bottom lip curled in under her teeth, and she pulled a handkerchief from her cardigan pocket to cover her mouth and hide her grief.

"If only . . ." The words came out ugly and twisted with grief. "If only she had fallen . . ."

She hunched forward, pushing her elbows into her belly, pressing the handkerchief over her mouth, her shoulders shaking convulsively, but in complete silence, until her voice broke free and she cried, "*Oh God! Oh God, dear Lord, if only she had fallen . . .!*"

Dehan rose and sat next to her, encircled her with her arms, and held her until the storm subsided. Mrs. Jones blew her nose and wiped streaks of wet mascara across her cheeks.

"I found her. She was lying on her face, with her legs slightly apart. It looked so strange, like she was just having a little rest. She had her coat open. I remember thinking she'd catch cold. And then I saw the big stain. We only have one streetlamp on Pugsley Avenue, and it was across from where she was lying, but it was enough to see the blood. She'd been stabbed with a big pair of scissors, right in the middle of her back. There was lots of . . . lots of blood. And when I looked at her face, her eyes were open, just looking across the sidewalk at the wall. She looked surprised, more than anything else."

She unfolded her handkerchief and examined it for a while, as though it really was interesting. When she spoke again, she was frowning at the handkerchief. "She was lying right outside Pat and Cyril's house, just past their gate."

CHAPTER 2

We stepped out into the frosted street. The trees, naked and cold, reached twiggy fingers toward an unfriendly, gunmetal-gray sky, weighed low with sagging clouds. The roofs of the odd jumble of houses that was Pugsley Avenue were lightly dusted with snow, and small drifts had accumulated beside chimney pots, against garden walls and car tires.

Dehan shuddered beside me as she looked up at the bellying menace of the clouds and pulled her coat close about her throat. She had on a woolly hat with a pom-pom, and I noted that her cheeks and the tip of her nose had turned pink, but I made no comment.

It was no more than thirty yards from Mrs. Jones' house to Cyril Perkins' house. To our left a road sign reading *END* stood before a wall of trees that was the southernmost end of Pugsley Creek Park. We stepped onto the icy blacktop and walked with care. There was no sidewalk at that section of the avenue, and the road surface was slippery with black ice.

Cyril Perkins' house was an ugly, three-story gabled affair in beige stone. A flight of nine steps formed a dogleg up to a porch that sat above a narrow basement window. We climbed the cold, concrete steps, and Dehan rang the bell while she stamped her feet, then breathed condensation into her woolen gloves. When he didn't open straightaway, she rapped on the wood with her knuckles, and a small voice came from inside, saying the owner was coming.

The door opened a moment later to reveal a small man with amused blue eyes. He had thin hair on a round head, reading glasses suspended on a chain around his neck, and a cardigan that had become lost somewhere between green and beige sometime in the early 1950s. His plaid, fur-lined slippers said he was not going to be taking swift action over anything anytime soon. There was a sweet aroma of pipe tobacco lingering on the air.

I showed him my badge, and Dehan fumbled hers out of her pocket with woolen fingers.

"Good afternoon, I am Detective John Stone of the NYPD, this is Detective Dehan. May we have a word with you about your wife, Patricia Perkins?"

His eyes went wide, and his eyebrows rose up his forehead. I thought he looked worried. "Have you found her? Is she all right?"

Dehan answered. "No, Mr. Perkins, we haven't found her yet. But it is *very* cold out here . . ."

He blinked once, then stood back, pulling the door open with him. "Of course! Of course! Please, come into the parlor where it is warm. I have a fire burning. It is a wicked day. Will you have some coffee?"

"Yes!" It was Dehan. She glanced at me as we stepped through the door into the living room and added, "Please. That would be nice."

What he called the parlor was a large, long room with two windows overlooking a backyard with a vegetable patch and tall trees that towered over the house. The drapes were half-drawn, to allow in light but keep out the cold. To the left a dark dining table stood on a dark, wooden floor, and beyond it a door gave on to a kitchen that had been modern 'round about the time his cardigan was knitted.

To the right there was a large fireplace where he had logs burning over smokeless coals. The walls were a dull cream with large, framed prints of famous Impressionist paintings. An ancient, heavy, three-piece suite in dark green was ranged around the fire. His chair was easily identified by the occasional table beside it that held a cup, a book by Steinbeck, and an old ashtray with a pipe sitting in it.

He paused in the middle of the floor, took our coats, and gestured at the suite with both hands.

"Please, sit. I will be but a couple of minutes. Make yourselves comfortable and, above all, warm!"

I went and lowered myself into an armchair while Dehan leaned over the fireplace, warming her hands while the orange light bathed her face. After a while she stood with her back to the flames and mouthed at me, *No Christmas decorations!*

I made a face that said maybe he'd lost his taste for that kind of thing. That can happen when your wife kills your neighbor with a pair of scissors on Christmas Day.

She cocked her head and made a kind of shrug with her head that said maybe I had a point at that.

Cyril Perkins came out of the kitchen with a green wooden tray laden with coffee, cream, sugar, and Christmas pudding. He settled himself in his chair, set the tray on the table with an air of satisfaction, and set about pouring the coffee and sharing it out, like Santa handing out presents. As he served the pudding and handed it to Dehan, he said, "So you are not here to tell me you have found Pat."

Dehan helped herself to cream in her coffee and on the pudding and stuffed a surprising amount into her mouth. After that she said, "M'fwaid nodg, Mshta Pwkinsh."

I nodded and smiled at her and said, "I'm afraid not, Mr. Perkins. I head up a cold-cases unit at the Forty-Third, and though this case is only a year old . . ."

His eyebrows shot up, and he pierced me with very bright blue eyes. "Only?"

I nodded. "Forgive my choice of words. Working homicide can make you a little callous at times. I assure you we take every case extremely seriously. My partner and I have worked cases that were twenty and thirty years old. As cold cases go, one year is comparatively recent. For you, of course, it is quite different."

He seemed to study my face for a moment, blinked a couple of times, and returned to his coffee. "I understand that," he said, "but it has been a very long year." He sipped. "So the case has gone cold, and it has been passed to you."

"Yes. We have all the background, we have the reports from the ME and the investigating team at the time . . ." I tasted the pudding. It was extremely good. I sipped the coffee. It was also extremely good. As I set down the cup I said, "But as a methodology it seems to me unwise to start your investigation on the same foundations of a prior investigation which failed to produce results."

He wiped his mouth on a paper napkin and smiled warmly at me. "One is led to believe that the police, or the cops, should I say, are hard-boiled, unimaginative, and lacking in human depth. But your thinking is almost philosophical. That is good. So you, Detective Stone, like to go right back to the beginning and look at everything with fresh eyes. The evidence—or what is left of it—has not changed, but the perception of the investigator has. So, what would you like to know?"

Dehan struggled to swallow, but I beat her to the question. "What was it about Lilith that Pat hated so much?"

He set down his cup and saucer with great care and dabbed at his lips again.

"It is perception again, isn't it? I don't believe she hated Lilith, I believe she hated herself and projected her hatred onto Lilith, because Lilith was everything that she wanted to be and felt unable to become. She didn't know, or didn't care, that I loved her for what she was. It wasn't . . ." He wrinkled his eyes in a smile. "As people are so fond of saying these days, it wasn't *about* me. Pat was the issue: her self-loathing, her anger, her inability to rise above the limitations of her appetites and her fat, her unrelenting belief that problems could be solved instantly, at the stroke of an angry phone call, a fit of rage . . . or a pair of scissors."

All trace of his earlier smile had faded to an expression of infinite sadness. "I had no desire for her to be like Lilith. Lilith would have bored me to distraction, charming and beautiful as she was. But the tragedy was that Pat had never really loved me, or anyone else for that matter. Pat saw the world as a place where she had to impose her ego at all costs. It was as though her very survival depended on it. I was no more than another possession which she used or deployed at will in the service of her own self-aggrandizement. She was the queen, the empress, of the universe, and any who crossed her or defied her were dealt with in no uncertain terms."

Dehan had stopped eating and drinking and had been watching him carefully. Now she cleared her throat and arched an eyebrow at him.

"I'm a little confused . . ."

He laughed with genuine amusement and leaned back in his chair. "I am not surprised, Detective Dehan!"

She didn't pause. "You claim that you loved her as she was and that you didn't want her to change, and yet you describe her as . . ."

For a moment she was lost for words and shrugged. He said, "An abominable woman."

She nodded. "Yes, really. I mean, you make her sound awful." She shook her head and shrugged. "So what was to love?"

He sighed, not with impatience, but with the effort of putting into words something which was inexplicable. Eventually he said, "Are you familiar with Iris Murdoch, Detective Dehan?"

"I know the name . . ."

"She was one of the great writers of the twentieth century, a real intellectual, a Buddhist, an existentialist, deeply in love with Jean-Paul . . ." He smiled, closed his eyes, and shook his head. "I digress. I could hear Pat right then: 'Here we go, sit down, ladies and gentlemen, for the great lecture!'"

He picked up his pipe, examined it a moment, and set it down again. "In *The Sea, The Sea*, she writes a fascinating portrait of a man who is incapable of understanding the relationship between the woman he loves and her husband. And the point is that what connects people is not what they like about each other. It is the needs they satisfy in each other that bind them. And Pat, for all her ill humor, her egotism, and occasional cruelty, satisfied deep needs in me. Detective, I have no shame in admitting that she gave me security. She made me feel safe, and I miss her every day. Every night I pray that she will come back to me, and that we will be able to prove her innocence in this appalling affair." He glanced at Dehan and laughed out loud at the expression on her face. "Love," he said, "is no more than need, Detective Dehan. Love is just need."

I sipped my coffee and set down the cup. "That is a little beyond our remit..."

"And yet it is at the heart of every motive for murder since people started murdering each other."

"You're probably right, Mr. Perkins, but I'm afraid we need to stick with concrete facts. Could you outline for us, please, the events of that day? I believe you had your wife's brother staying with you..."

He gave a small grunt and nodded. "Ernest, or as he is popularly known, Ern. Yes, Pat insisted he should be there every Christmas. It was not so much a case of being charitable to him—I am quite sure he could have had much nicer Christmases than he enjoyed with us—it was more a case of exercising control over him, or perhaps more to the point, of having a group of dependent people gathered around her, praising her and receiving her bounty."

I said, "You're pretty scathing about her, Mr. Perkins."

He chuckled. "Don't read too much into that, Detective Stone. I am sarcastic by nature. I had a reputation for it among the boys, and my fellow teachers were well aware of it. They used to call me Ascorbic Cyril." He shrugged and gave his head a little shake. "I can't pretend that I liked Pat. There was very little to like. But I did love her very dearly. She fulfilled me somehow, and as I said, I pray nightly for her return."

Dehan broke in, "Okay, so Ern was here. Was there anybody else?"

"No, just the three of us."

"And what was the deal with Ern and Lilith?"

"The deal . . ."

He gazed into the flames, absently picked up his pipe, and started to fill it with a strong, sweet tobacco. He took his time lighting it with two long tapers, which he shook out and tossed into the hot embers.

"Not to put too fine a point on it, Detective Dehan, Ern was obsessed with Lilith. Of course we and the Joneses have been neighbors for years, and we had watched Lilith grow from a baby into a fine young lady. Her mother was, and indeed is, somewhat peculiar, but she was a very good mother and raised a very lovely daughter. You may not think so to look at me, Detectives, but I have a gift with children. I have worked with children all my adult life, and for some reason they seem to like me. Lilith was no different. Gwen—that's Mrs. Jones—and I would often stop for a chat, especially after her husband died, and little Lilith would always be with her, naturally, and as the child began to grow and develop intellectually, we developed the kind of friendship that grows between a child and a favored uncle."

"Did you visit with them?"

"No." He shook his head firmly. "No, not at first, but when Lilith was about ten, and it began to become clear that Gwen would probably remain single, they both began to invite me over occasionally for tea and cakes, and that sort of thing. I think it was nice for Gwen to have a male figure around, albeit an uncleish one, to help out with a few small things like changing a plug or writing a stern letter to the bank."

He gave a small, self-deprecating smile.

"Not surprisingly, Pat was not very amused by my occasional visits to the Joneses' house. At first she did little more than grumble, as the invites tended to take the form of a request for help followed by an offer of coffee and chocolate brownies. But as we became more familiar, closer, the invites themselves also became more relaxed in nature. It might be that Lilith had a presentation at school: Would I like to watch her dress rehearsal? Or celebrate the fact that it had gone well!

"When the nature of the invites changed, then Pat began to resent them more. That was when she started to insist on Ern visiting us on a regular basis, and once he was here, she would find every conceivable pretext to send him over to the Joneses'. It might be to borrow a cup of sugar, to *return* a pound of sugar . . ."

Dehan was frowning, scratching her shiny black head. "What was the purpose of sending Ern over . . ."

He smiled, then gave a small laugh. "Well, primarily to sabotage any intimate friendship that might be developing between Gwen and myself, but also in the hope that, as Lilith began to develop as a young woman, Ern would fall in love with her."

"She *wanted* Ern to fall in love with Lilith?"

"Oh, certainly!" He laughed. "That way Pat could cause extreme discomfort to Gwen and Lilith, make my presence undesirable by association, and guarantee herself an excuse to go barging over there anytime she wanted to and burst in on whatever she imagined was happening."

I said, "And that was, in fact, what happened on that Christmas Day."

He seemed not to hear and went on, speaking softly. "The thing was, Ern did in fact become obsessed with Lilith. He was . . ." He sucked in his lips and shook his head at the fire. "We are so precious these days, so afraid of offending, that we have forgotten often it is the truth that offends. The Spanish call them subnormal; we used to call them mentally retarded. Today we have to say that they have learning difficulties. But the fact remains that a rose by any other name is the same flower. However precious and anally retentive we care to be, Ern was both subnormal and mentally retarded. He was simple and had the mentality of a five-year-old child. It was a congenital condition. Both of their parents were mental retards. When I tell you that Pat was the intelligent one in the family, you will get some idea of what they were like."

Dehan was frowning hard. "So, does Pat have mental health issues?"

He puffed at his pipe, watching her for a moment. "Mental health issues? Another one of those sanitized, modern expressions. Her IQ was bang on one hundred. What most people don't realize is that one hundred, the average, is not even bright. It is dull, unimaginative, simple. And that was her. She had a certain low cunning about her, but she was not bright. She saw things in black-and-white terms of what was right or wrong according to her principles, and her principles were mainly shaped by what she wanted or didn't want.

"Whether she was in any way traumatized by her parents, I am not sure. Whether she was neurotic, I am not sure. She was certainly not psychotic. I think she was quite simply greedy and not very bright."

"That's another pretty harsh assessment, Mr. Perkins."

"Is it? Life is harsh. Reality is harsh, Detective Stone. She was born of mentally retarded parents and had a mentally retarded brother; it was a miracle she was not herself a mental retard. She had the good fortune to meet a man who loved her, who was able to value and treasure those aspects of her personality which were beautiful and valuable."

Dehan raised an eyebrow. "What are those aspects? We haven't heard anything about them yet."

He answered without hesitation. "She was a wonderful, loving mother. She was . . ." He thought a moment, then laughed. "She was *abundant*, generous, giving, like a primal force of nature. When she was not angry, she was delightful. She was strong, uncompromising, pure, and raw. I have an IQ of one hundred and fifty-five, Detectives, and she would often shake her head and say, 'I don't know what you see in me, Cyril,' and I would tell her that was because she was simple, and we would both laugh. I could never explain to her why I loved her, nor did she really want to know. It was enough that I did love her. But for me it was a fascination—an intoxication—with those primal forces that were so powerfully abundant in her."

I scratched my chin. "You say she was a wonderful mother . . ."

"Superb."

"You have a daughter, right?"

"Theresa." He smiled. "Fortunately she inherited my brains and the good side of her mother's nature. She is a very talented young doctor at the Harlem Hospital, and much of what she has achieved is down to her mother's diligence and hard work."

We fell silent for a moment. I gazed at the dancing flames and felt momentarily sleepy in the close, warm room.

"Can you tell us what happened that day, Mr. Perkins?"

He nodded several times. "I can tell you exactly what happened that day."

CHAPTER 3

"Theresa was working that week. This is the sacrifice that doctors make. Their life is not their own. It belongs to their patients. Or to the hospital that employs them. But I digress. Pat had insisted once again on having Ern stay with us. He had a small apartment near Hunts Point where he lived a squalid, unhappy, lonely life. I confess that about three hundred and fifty days of the year we paid very little attention to him, and I would happily have ignored him the remaining fifteen days, but Pat had some qua-religious idea that if she was nice to him at Christmas she would somehow qualify as a good person, despite the way she treated him the rest of the year. That was Pat's simplistic way of thinking: the rule is, be kind at Christmas, so that was what she did.

"She had sent me over Christmas Eve in the morning to collect him. I knew from the start that he was going to be a nuisance because he had bought Lilith a whole bag of presents. Mainly they consisted of plastic bead necklaces and bracelets, and cheap perfume from the local drugstore. There were also pictures he had cut out from magazines—pictures of horses, or sunsets, or forests in New England in the fall, you know the sort of thing.

"I advised him that maybe it wasn't such a great idea to overwhelm her with cheap presents, and maybe we could stop at a store and buy her one thing that we could be sure she would like, but he was adamant. These were his treasures for her.

"So, on Christmas morning, after we had given each other our presents under the tree, he bathed, shaved, and dressed and took himself down the road to the Joneses' house. Conversation at home, from that point on, between Pat and myself, was pretty limited. In fact, it was more of a monologue than a dialogue, a monologue in which she ranted about how the Joneses were precious and stuck-up, persnickety and narrow-minded, and how Ern was going to drive them crazy and they would never want to have anything to do with us ever again. She said all this, and repeated it over and over again, with a smug smile on her face. I think you would call that incongruent: her words expressed something regrettable, but her facial demeanor and her tone of voice displayed happiness and satisfaction."

He shrugged, then smiled. "She was, so to speak, weaponizing Ern in order to destroy what shreds of friendship remained between us, as families. However, by midday Ern had not been sent packing. On the contrary, he was still there, eating cake and drinking coffee, and chatting away to Lilith."

Dehan had been watching him through narrowed eyes. Now she reached behind her head and gathered up her abundant black hair, which had untied itself, and tied it into a knot again. As she did it, she said, "So you decided to go and join him?"

He gave his comfortable chuckle again, and his eyes actually seemed to twinkle. "If I am perfectly honest, I went over with the intention of bringing him home for lunch. Pat and I had been busy in the kitchen, but once there the atmosphere was so friendly and agreeable, so very different from the atmosphere I had left behind at my own home, that I allowed myself to be induced to stay."

Dehan arched a withering eyebrow. "Who induced you to stay?"

He didn't miss the implication of the question. "Ahhh . . . I am afraid, flattering as your question is, there was none of that. There are men, like George Clooney, Picasso, Clint Eastwood, who even in their later years retain a magnetic attraction for women. I am not one of those men. Even as a young man, Detective Dehan, women were not attracted to me. I haven't got 'it.' Gwen enjoyed my company and was fond of me, while Lilith and I had a friendship founded on having known each other for many years. I was like an uncle for her. Certainly at her tender years she had no other kind of interest in me." He paused, gazing at Dehan with amused eyes. "So in answer to your question, they both induced me to stay, but only through simple friendship, nothing more."

He paused a moment in thought, gazing at the hypnotic dance of the flames.

"I suppose we lost track of time, Ern indulging his besotted obsession with Lilith, and I enjoying the pleasant atmosphere of a happy home.

"I don't normally drink much, but we had a couple of eggnogs, and before I knew it, it was becoming dusk outside and there was a fearful banging at the door. Pat had come over and was raging. She rang the bell, beat the door, and demanded that Ern and I go outside. Dear Gwen, bless her, urged her to come inside, but the more agreeable Gwen tried to be, the more furious Pat became. Her language, I'm afraid, descended somewhat south of the gutter, and she accused Lilith of things that were quite unwarranted. She used various epithets that made Lilith out to be a prostitute and suggested, quite ridiculously, that Lilith was engaged in an illicit, adulterous relationship with me.

"In the end, between us, Ern and I managed to drag Pat home, and we left Lilith and Gwen to enjoy a quiet, belated Christmas luncheon together. Our own luncheon was not to be enjoyed. Pat was furious. It was hard to pin down exactly what she was furious about, but it seemed that she felt Gwen and Lilith Jones were out to steal her family from her. Her ranting and raving became so extreme and extravagant that Ernest, who is normally oblivious to most things, became quite upset, and no sooner had we finished eating than I packed him in the car and took him, well"—he hesitated a moment—"home."

I asked, "Was that unusual?"

"Oh yes, normally he would have stayed another few days, at least until New Year's, but Pat seemed exceptionally upset, and he was vulnerable. So I thought it wise to remove him from the situation. Besides, Theresa and I had arranged new, more comfortable lodgings for him, at the St. George's Clinic for the Vulnerable and At Risk. Pat knew nothing about it. She would never have approved."

He sat staring at the bowl of his pipe for a moment. His face was suddenly drawn and sallow. "To some extent I blame myself for what happened next. I think I had grown so accustomed to Pat's behavior, her constant complaining and sniping, that I had failed to notice it was getting worse."

He looked up, and I was struck by how direct his gaze was. "Of course I missed the times when we would laugh. She had an extraordinary sense of humor—not sophisticated or subtle, but huge. She would become helpless with laughter on seeing baby ducks staggering after their mother. I remember she was in bed one night, and I was undressing. I was telling her about my day at work, and I told her, 'The kids were fascinated by Uranus,' but I pronounced it the vulgar, popular way, as, 'your anus.' Well, if I said she was helpless with laughter for the next twenty minutes I would not be exaggerating. And for the next week, remembering it was enough to set her off again. She had a vast capacity for laughter." He paused, nodding. "I missed that, because her laughter had dried up, but it is also true that I had failed to read the signs of how bad she felt, how desolate and alone she must have felt."

Dehan said, "What happened?"

"I took Ernest home, told him I might return for him the next day, and drove back to Pat. But when I got home, Pat wasn't there." He puffed out his cheeks, closed his eyes, and blew. "I have been told, your first detective told me, that I walked right past where Lilith was lying. She was just twenty-five feet from where I passed. I have measured it. There is but one lamppost in this section of the avenue, and its light is largely filtered through the foliage of the trees. In December it was dark, clouded, and moonless." He shook his head. "But all the explanations in the world will never rid me of the feeling of horror and regret, that I walked past poor Lilith's body without seeing her.

"The first indication I had that something was wrong was when I realized that Pat's car was gone. It was a big Toyota RAV4; I assumed that she had gone for a drive to cool off. It struck me as odd and, I have to say, extremely out of character, but before I could give it much thought, I had gone inside the house.

"At first I didn't notice anything wrong. Everything seemed to be exactly as I had left it, except that there was an unearthly silence and . . ." He nodded and made a rueful smile. "It slowly dawned on me that the fact that everything was exactly as I had left it was, in itself, wrong. Pat was obsessive. She would have cleared the table, loaded the dishwasher, made coffee. But it was as though she had vanished from the face of the Earth the moment I had stepped outside the door. I checked the whole house and I called her on her cell, but I got no reply, and eventually her cell went dead."

He fell silent. I asked, "What did you do?"

"At first I had no idea *what* to do. It was so out of character! Then it occurred to me that maybe she had gone back to the Joneses' house, to take up with Lilith where she had left off. But the thought had no sooner crossed my mind than I heard those terrible screams. They will live with me for the rest of my life."

"What did you do?"

"I ran!"

"You ran?"

"I ran, out of the house and down the steps. It was dark, and it was sleeting. It was bizarre because for a moment all I could think about was how luminous the specks of sleet were in the darkness, and yet there was that terrible screaming going on. The human mind is strange like that. Then I ran down to the sidewalk and saw Gwen kneeling beside a dark bulk, shaking it and screaming."

He stopped dead, staring sidelong at the flames in the fireplace. We waited in a silence that almost rang in your ears; the crackle and spit of the fire seemed to slide across the face of that silence, without ever disturbing it. When he spoke again it was quite sudden.

"I hurried over. All sorts of crazy thoughts crossed my mind. I wondered if it was a dog that had been run over and wondered at the intensity of Gwen's grief over a dog. I even wondered if it was Pat. What never crossed my mind was that it might be Lilith. That never crossed my mind for a moment. How could anything like that happen? And when I . . ."

He stopped and stared at me. There was outrage in his eyes. He turned his stare on Dehan, as though we had both proposed something insane and offensive.

"When I saw that it was her. I thought . . ." He shook his head. "I thought she'd slipped, tripped, fallen . . . And then I began to see: her eyes were open, she was facedown, staring at the wall, the scissors poking grotesquely, obscenely out of her back, the blood; and you think, maybe it wasn't lethal, maybe she can still be saved. But you can see her eyes are open. And when Gwen shook her, it was horrific, like trying to shake putty . . ."

Dehan said, "You were fond of her."

"Very. Of course. I guess she was like a niece, only, as I had watched her grow up, and we had become friends, it was more than that."

"What happened next?"

"I can't remember who called the police. It may even have been me. My memory becomes very patchy at this point. I know very shortly after that our quiet street was full of flashing red-and-blue lights, and your detective was asking lots of questions about my wife and how she got on with Lilith." He gave a small laugh.

"You don't need to be Sherlock Holmes to see the implications, but"—he shook his head—"I still find it very hard to believe that Pat, for all that she was a very strong, angry woman, that she should be capable of killing. I find that very hard to accept."

I nodded for a few seconds, slowly, sucking my teeth. "The scissors?"

He sighed and screwed up his eyes, pinching the bridge of his nose. "Yes, yes, I know. They were from her sewing set, and they had her prints on them, as they naturally would, being hers!"

Dehan offered a humorless, lopsided smile. "But I think the important point, Mr. Perkins, is that they had nobody else's prints on them." He didn't open his eyes. He just nodded. She went on, "She took her car, and here's the part I am having trouble with, Mr. Perkins: nobody knew her better than you did, but you have no idea where she went. How is that possible?"

He sighed, then opened his eyes and flopped back in his chair.

"I can see how you would think that, but actually you are quite wrong. Did you know that statistically, fat people are more likely to be secretive than thin or normal-weight people?"

"No, I didn't know that."

"Well, it was certainly true of Pat. Everything in her life was on a need-to-know basis, and nobody needed to know anything, except her. She was obsessive about it. She'd tell you they weren't secrets, but that nobody had any business knowing anything about her private life. Sometimes it was stupid things like whether she had bought lamb or chicken for dinner. Other times it was more intimate, private stuff, like not wanting to put her underwear on the line to dry, so the neighbors wouldn't know what kind of underwear she wore."

Dehan sighed. "So you have no idea where Pat would have run to?"

He gave a small sigh of exasperation and spread his hands. "Logically she would have gone to her brother. But that was clearly out of the question. So where *could* she go? Your detective immediately acquired access to her bank accounts and her credit cards, and as far as I know he discovered no movement on any of them."

I grunted. "But you said at the time that her clothes were missing?"

"Oh yes, well, that is to say, her favorite clothes, not all of them. She had recently bought some rather fancy pieces that were quite flattering, considering her size. She had also taken to buying more expensive makeup, and that was missing too. Her toothbrush, her toothpaste, all her toiletries were gone."

I gave my head a scratch, not because it itched, but because I was embarrassed. I had asked the question of a thousand husbands over the years, but there was something about Cyril Perkins that made the question somehow insolent, even outrageous.

"Mr. Perkins, is it possible that your wife was having an affair?"

There was real amusement in his smile and in his eyes.

"I would say that was highly unlikely."

"What makes it unlikely, Mr. Perkins?"

"I don't want to be indelicate, but she was not the most attractive woman in the world. I suppose her face was pretty, when she was smiling, which was admittedly not often. But she weighed two hundred and sixty pounds, and her personality wasn't exactly charming."

Dehan was frowning. "You married her..."

"Oh, yes, I did. Um... How can I put this? I am not exactly Hugh Jackman, or for that matter George Clooney. My first wife, I will admit freely, was a mail-order Philippine woman who actually left me and returned to the Philippines. Pat met me shortly after that, demanded sex, got pregnant, and obliged me to marry her."

"Obliged you how?"

"By appealing to my sense of morals and ethics, of course. And my reputation in the neighborhood. I am a good Catholic, Detective."

Dehan gave her head a series of little shakes, like she was clearing it. "You married her because of your reputation in the neighborhood, and because you are a Catholic?"

"Those were both factors, but not the only factors. There was also the fact that I had got her pregnant. I had a duty to care for that child." He took a deep breath and sighed. "And there was also the fact that I did not sincerely believe I would ever find anybody else. She clearly wanted to make a family with me . . ."

The shrug and the silence that followed were eloquent.

I put my hands on my knees and glanced at Dehan. Her eyebrows said she'd run out of questions, so I stood. I was about to tell him we'd let him get on when a photograph caught my eye on the mantelshelf. It was the street outside, with the Joneses' house in the background. There was a light scattering of snow, and a very pretty girl with blond hair, wrapped in a big fur coat, was standing, smiling, next to a big guy who was grinning from ear to considerable ear. He had one arm around her and was squeezing too tight. On the other side of the blonde was another girl holding on to her arm. She was also pretty, but not as glamorous.

I picked up the photograph and showed it to him. "Lilith and Ern?" He nodded. "Lilith is the blonde. The other girl is our daughter, Theresa."

"Mind if we take a picture?"

"Of course, be my guest."

Dehan took a photograph and set it back on the fireplace. We shook hands with Cyril Perkins and made our way out of his house and down the stairs to the bracing, icy cold of the street.

Scan the QR code below to purchase A CHRISTMAS KILLING.
Or go to: righthouse.com/a-christmas-killing

Printed in Dunstable, United Kingdom